THE HARSH TRUTH OF THE BULLET

When you've lived by the gun for as long as Clint Adams had, certain sounds become familiar. One was the sound of a hammer being cocked on a gun. Because of that sound, when Irons stepped out into the open and started bringing his gun around, Clint only had to pull the trigger of his own weapon to send a bullet into the man's chest. He reacted the same way his partner had: he stepped back, arms windmilling, a shocked look on his face, blood spurting from his chest—only he tripped over his fallen compadre and fell on top of him.

The two men were dead—and stacked like firewood.

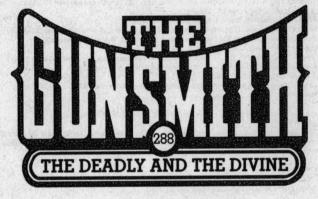

THE GUNSMITH

288

THE DEADLY AND THE DIVINE

J. R. ROBERTS

JOVE BOOKS, NEW YORK

THE BERKLEY PUBLISHING GROUP
Published by the Penguin Group
Penguin Group (USA) Inc.
375 Hudson Street, New York, New York 10014, USA
Penguin Group (Canada), 90 Eglinton Avenue East, Suite 700, Toronto, Ontario M4P 2Y3, Canada
(a division of Pearson Penguin Canada Inc.)
Penguin Books Ltd., 80 Strand, London WC2R 0RL, England
Penguin Group Ireland, 25 St. Stephen's Green, Dublin 2, Ireland (a division of Penguin Books Ltd.)
Penguin Group (Australia), 250 Camberwell Road, Camberwell, Victoria 3124, Australia
(a division of Pearson Australia Group Pty. Ltd.)
Penguin Books India Pvt. Ltd., 11 Community Centre, Panchsheel Park, New Delhi—110 017, India
Penguin Group (NZ), Cnr. Airborne and Rosedale Roads, Albany, Auckland 1310, New Zealand
(a division of Pearson New Zealand Ltd.)
Penguin Books (South Africa) (Pty.) Ltd., 24 Sturdee Avenue, Rosebank, Johannesburg 2196,
South Africa

Penguin Books Ltd., Registered Offices: 80 Strand, London WC2R 0RL, England

This is a work of fiction. Names, characters, places, and incidents either are the product of the author's imagination or are used fictitiously, and any resemblance to actual persons, living or dead, business establishments, events, or locales is entirely coincidental.

THE DEADLY AND THE DIVINE

A Jove Book / published by arrangement with the author

PRINTING HISTORY
Jove edition / December 2005

ISBN: 0-515-14044-9

JOVE®
Jove Books are published by The Berkley Publishing Group,
a division of Penguin Group (USA) Inc.,
375 Hudson Street, New York, New York 10014.
JOVE is a registered trademark of Penguin Group (USA) Inc.
The "J" design is a trademark belonging to Penguin Group (USA) Inc.

PRINTED IN THE UNITED STATES OF AMERICA

10 9 8 7 6 5 4 3 2 1

ONE

Clint sat in the audience and enjoyed the performance that was taking place on stage. The play was mediocre, which pretty much matched the cast, except for the star. As usual, Sarah Bernhardt lived up to her reputation. She outshone the material and everyone on stage with her. It was the first time Clint had ever seen "the Divine Sarah" on stage, and he was impressed.

When the play was finished he walked up to the stage and gave his name to the security man there, who allowed him to pass without comment. When he got backstage he found it was wall-to-wall people. Not a good situation if you were worried about someone's safety. He scanned the crowd for any sign of his friend, Jack Gallows. He was in Cleveland and at the Cleveland Arts Theater at the behest of Gallows, who was a private detective with offices in New York and Chicago. Gallows had just recently left the prestigious Pinkerton Agency to start his own business. He had sent a telegram to Clint asking him to meet him in Cleveland on urgent business. He also told Clint to leave his horse home. There weren't many men who could have summoned him that way—perhaps half a dozen—and Gallows was one of them.

After a few moments he spotted Gallows in the crowd, which wasn't difficult. At six-four, he pretty much towered over the rest of the crowd. Slowly, he made his way over to where his friend was standing.

"Jack!"

Gallows's head swiveled around at the sound of his name and he grinned broadly when he saw Clint making his way to him. He started toward Clint at the same time and suddenly the crowd parted before the big man.

He greeted Clint with his hand out.

"It's great to see you," he said, shaking Clint's hand vigorously. "Thanks for coming."

"I got here as quickly as I could," Clint said. "Your telegram said it was urgent."

"It is," Gallows said, "but we can't talk here. Meet me in the bar at my hotel at eleven. Is that all right?"

"Sure, but why did you want me to come here tonight?"

"I'll tell you that when we meet later," Gallows said. "I'm at the Cleveland House."

No matter where he went, what city or town, there was always a hotel with the word *house* in the name. He couldn't really complain about that, though, since one of his favorite hotels was the Denver House in Denver. The Cleveland House was only two blocks from the hotel he was staying in, The Cumberland.

"Well . . . all right," Clint said. "Is there anything I can do for you here?"

"No," Jack Gallows said, "I've got it covered here. We'll talk later." The big detective grabbed Clint's hand again. "Thanks again for comin', Clint."

"Sure, Jack, sure," Clint said. He wanted to say more, but suddenly the crowd closed around them and the big man was gone.

Clint turned to work his way through the crowd to get out,

but as he did a man bumped into him and moved on without a word of apology. Clint turned to watch the man, who was swallowed up by the sea of people. He wasn't sure who all these people were—guests, the press, well-wishers—but this man did not seem to fit in. He was dressed well enough, but looked uncomfortable in his clothes. Also, it was a cool night, and the man was sweating profusely.

And then there was the gun.

Clint had felt the gun beneath the man's jacket when he passed. For a night at the theater a gun was not usually required attire—even though he, himself, had one. He was wearing his Colt New Line tucked into his belt at the small of his back, but that was because with his rep it was not healthy for him to go out without it.

Abruptly, he reversed his direction and started after the man.

George Bagby was a nervous wreck.

He had never killed anyone before, but this had to be done. This was a debt that was owed, and he had to pay it, no matter what. Even if it cost him his own life.

The crowd closed in around him, and he jostled people as he went, drawing looks of both annoyance and anger, but he didn't care. He kept his mind focused, even though he was sweating inside his ill-fitting suit. The perspiration wasn't from the suit, though, but from his nerves. He could feel the clamminess of his hands and kept rubbing them dry on his trousers. He hoped the gun would not slip from his hand when the time came to pull the trigger.

As he approached his prey he reached inside his jacket for the gun, a Navy Colt he'd bought just recently from a gun shop. It had been cheap because it was not in very good condition, but the man had assured him that it would fire—at least once—without exploding or coming apart in his hand. The gun had ridden uncomfortably on his hip this whole time, tucked into his belt, but now he closed his hand around the butt, slid his finger into the trigger guard, drew the gun, cocked it and pointed—

"I don't think so," someone said in his ear, and a hand closed over the gun, the web between the thumb and forefinger keeping the hammer from doing its job.

TWO

In the bar at the Cleveland House, Clint Adams shook his hand again. It was still sore where it had been pinched when the hammer of George Bagby's Navy Colt had come down on it.

"You sure you don't want to go to a doctor?" Jack Gallows asked.

"For this? No," Clint said. "I'll just have another beer—on you. That'll help it feel okay."

Luckily, it was his left hand, and not his gun hand.

"Well, you sure did me a favor already," Gallows said. "Bagby would have put a bullet in me for sure and probably some innocent bystanders."

"Not with that gun," Clint said. "One shot and it would have been useless. But you would have been dead, which, I guess, was the point. Who was he?"

"I put his brother away a year ago when I was here on a case," Gallows said.

"And he waited all this time to take his revenge?"

Gallows shrugged and said, "I guess he had to wait until I came back here. He didn't have the money to come and find me."

"I guess he barely had the money to buy the suit and the gun," Clint said. "Did you turn him over to the police?"

"I couldn't," Gallows said. "I let him go. He was blubberin' so much."

"Do you think that was such a good idea, Jack?" Clint asked. "What if he comes after you again?"

"He'd have to get the money to buy another gun," Gallows said. "We'll be gone by then."

"We will?"

"Tomorrow's our last day here."

"And then where do you go?"

"Well," Gallows said, "I was hoping that we would be goin' to Chicago, together."

"And what's in Chicago?"

"Another stop on the Sarah Bernhardt tour," Gallows said.

"Ah, now we get to why you had me go to the theater."

"I wanted you to see her."

"Miss Bernhardt?"

Gallows nodded.

"I've been hired to keep her safe while she's on tour."

"How many more stops are there?"

"I'd have to ask her manager," he said, "but at least . . . lemme see . . . Chicago, St. Louis, Kansas City, Oklahoma City . . . Denver for sure . . ."

"Okay, I get it," Clint said. "Where did she start?"

"New York."

"That figures. What do you want from me, Jack?"

"I want you to work for me," he said. "I want you to guard her."

"That's your job."

"I'm a little shorthanded," Gallows said. "That's the only reason Bagby got that close to me with a gun."

"Shorthanded," Clint said. "How many men are you working with?"

"One," Gallows said.

"One?"

Gallows nodded and said, "Me."

"What about now?" Clint asked. "Who's watching her now?"

"I've been using locals when I get to a city," Gallows explained. "Got one in front of her door right now, but I don't always trust them. Clint, I need somebody I can really trust, and that's you."

"There's nobody else?"

"Well, Tal Roper," Gallows said, "but he's my second choice."

Clint had met Talbot Roper the same time he'd met Jack Gallows, when they were both working for Pinkerton. Roper had gone out on his own first, establishing himself in Denver, and was now considered one of the best private investigators in the country, if not the world. He was also one of Clint's closest friends and one of the men he'd trust with his life—along with men like Wyatt Earp, Bat Masterson, Luke Short . . . and Jack Gallows.

It had taken Gallows much longer to decide to go out on his own, and given the popularity of Sarah Bernhardt, this was a big job for one man to have taken on.

"How'd you get this job?" Clint asked.

"Believe it or not my old boss recommended me for it."

"William? Or Robert?"

"William."

Allan Pinkerton had died several years before, and his sons William and Robert had pretty much divvied the agency up, fifty-fifty.

"That's odd."

"It is," Gallows said. "I even thought that maybe he was setting me up to fail, but then I thought even he wouldn't want Sarah Bernhardt to be harmed or killed while she was here."

"I think you're probably right."

"So that leaves us with he did it out of the goodness of his heart?" Clint asked.

Gallows laughed and said, "There's got to be another reason, but I'm being paid too well to care. Well enough to pay you well."

"I thought you were asking me for a favor."

"No," Gallows said, "I'm asking you to work for me, Clint. I want you to be the inside man, while I'm the outside man. I'm asking you to be Sarah Bernhardt's personal bodyguard."

THREE

"I'd have to meet her," Clint said, later. They were sitting outside, in front of the hotel, each with a cigar.

"Of course."

"She might not like me."

"Women like you, Clint," Gallows said. "They've always liked you. Has that changed?"

"God, I hope not."

"And you still like them?"

"Very much."

"Then I think the two of you will get along."

"Still . . . I should meet her and get her approval, I think," he said. "Just to make sure we'll get along."

"I'll introduce you tomorrow."

"Good."

"Then you'll take the job?"

"I think I'll reserve my decision until after she and I meet," Clint said. "If that's okay?"

"That's fine," Gallows said. He took a last drag from his cigar, then flicked the remainder out into the street. "I'm going to check with my man and then turn in. Breakfast here, in the morning?"

"Sure."

"Nine A.M."

"I'll be here."

Gallows put his hand out and Clint shook it.

"Damned good of you to come, especially since all you thought I wanted was a favor."

"Can't travel too far to do a favor for a friend, Jack."

"I may have counted on that, Clint," Gallows said. "I'm sorry. I don't want you to think I take our friendship for granted."

"You don't have to apologize, Jack," Clint said. "I'll see you in the morning."

"Good night."

Gallows went into his hotel, and Clint started down the street toward his, still smoking his cigar.

Gallows went upstairs to Sarah Bernhardt's room. Sitting on a chair in front of her door was Harry Donnelly, a local private detective.

"Harry."

" 'Evenin', Mr. Gallows."

"Everything okay here?" Gallows asked.

"Seems to be quiet."

"I'll just check with Miss Bernhardt."

Donnelly moved aside and Gallows knocked. After a few moments the door opened and there she stood, the Divine Sarah. She looked smaller offstage, and wore much less makeup, but she was no less beautiful.

"Mr. Gallows."

"Miss Bernhardt," Gallows said. "I'm just checking to make sure everything is all right."

"Everything is fine, sir," she said. "I was just getting ready to retire for the evening."

"I just wanted to let you know . . . I have someone I want you to meet tomorrow."

"Oh?"

"A man I'm hiring, or hope to hire, to be your personal bodyguard."

"I thought that was you, Mr. Gallows."

"I can't be with you every moment, ma'am," he said. "The man I'm hoping to hire is also a friend of mine."

"Someone you trust?"

"Implicitly."

"Then I shall be glad to meet him," she said.

"I can bring him here in the afternoon," Gallows said, "and the two of you can talk."

She smiled and said, "I see. You want to see if I approve of him, or if he approves of me?"

"Both, I think."

"Very well," she said. "Noon?"

"That would be fine."

"Good night, then," she said.

"Good night, ma'am."

She closed the door gently, and Donnelly moved his chair back in front of it.

"Good night, Harry."

"Night, sir."

Gallows went down the hall several doors and into his own room.

Clint entered his room, turned up the gas lamp on the wall and locked the door behind him. He had come all this way, never expecting that he'd be meeting one of the most famous actresses in the theater. He'd met Lillie Langtry on several occasions and considered her to be a friend. She was, perhaps, the American version of Sarah Bernhardt. He wondered if the two women had ever seen each other perform, and if so, what they thought of each other.

Tomorrow, he thought as he got ready for bed, he'd get to ask one of them.

FOUR

Clint arrived at the dining room of the Cleveland House hotel at eight-fifty and Jack Gallows was already there, enjoying a cup of coffee.

"You're early," Gallows said.

"You're earlier," Clint said, sitting opposite him. He picked up the pot of coffee from the table and poured himself a cup.

"I didn't order yet," Gallows said. "Figured I'd wait for you."

The waiter came over at that point and Clint asked Gallows, "This is on you?"

"Yes."

"Steak and eggs," he told the waiter.

Gallows sighed and said, "Me, too."

The waiter went off to fill the orders.

"I talked to Miss Bernhardt last night," Gallows said. "Told her I'd be bringin' you up to meet her."

"How did she react?"

"Favorably," Gallows said. "She's very cooperative. Not at all what I expected."

"What did you expect?"

13

"That she'd be difficult," the detective said. "I mean, her reputation and all . . ."

"Reputations can be deceiving," Clint said.

"Obviously."

Clint didn't know if Gallows was referring to Sarah Bernhardt or him.

"Are you carrying a gun?" Gallows asked.

"Yes."

"Not on your hip, obviously."

"No."

"Shoulder rig?"

Clint shook his head.

"Don't like them," he said. "I've just got it tucked into my belt."

"That Colt New Line?"

"That's the one."

"Small caliber."

"I usually hit what I shoot at."

"I've got a cut down Colt in a shoulder rig," Gallows said. "Peacemaker."

"Nice."

"I can get you one . . . if you take the job."

"If I take the job I'll wear my own Colt," Clint said. "I'm kind of used to it."

"Okay," Gallows sad. "I want you to be comfortable."

The waiter arrived with their plates and Gallows asked him to bring a fresh pot of coffee.

"So, this job," Clint said. "Would I be guarding her against anyone in particular?"

"No," Gallows said. "Not that I've been told. Her manager just wanted her to be safe."

"Her manager?"

"Yeah, he's travelling with her," Gallows said. "You'll be meeting him as well."

"Does he have to approve me?"

"No," Gallows said. "That'll be up to her."

"What time will I be seeing her?"

"Noon."

"Gives me some time to kill."

"Eat slower," Gallows suggested.

Clint laughed, popped a piece of meat into his mouth.

"So how long have you been on your own?"

"A year."

"How's it going?"

"Not that well," Gallows admitted. "This is the first big paying job I've had. Everything else has been sort of . . . low class."

"Any other referrals from the Pinkerton?"

"No," Gallows said. "A couple from Tal Roper, though."

"I'd have sent some work your way if I knew you were on your own," Clint said.

"Well," Gallows said, "now you know."

They finished their breakfast amid small talk and worked their way through yet a third pot of coffee. By the time they were finished and paying the bill they still had an hour before meeting with the actress. They decided to take a walk outside.

"What's the manager like?" Clint asked.

"Very British," Gallows said. "Have you known many of them?"

"Some," Clint said. "I've been there."

"To England?"

"Yes."

"What for?"

"A gun show," Clint said. "It was years ago." He didn't mention the strangler he'd ended up helping to catch.

They walked completely around the hotel, and when they came around to the front again Gallows touched Clint on the arm and said, "There he is."

"There who is?"

"The manager, John Randolph Burton . . . oh, the third."

"The third?" Clint asked. "There's three of him?"

"Come on," Gallows said, "I'll just introduce you to one of them."

FIVE

John Randolph Burton was in his mid-forties, a small, well-dressed man with a bowler hat and silver-headed cane. When he spotted Gallows on the street he waved a hand and hurried toward him.

"Mr. Gallows, sir," Burton said. "Just the man I was looking for. I understand there was an incident at the theater last night."

"Nothing to worry about, Mr. Burton."

"Nothing to worry about? I heard there was a man with a gun—"

"There was, but Mr. Adams here stopped him before he could even draw it," Gallows said, "and the man was never anywhere near Miss Bernhardt's dressing room."

"This man thwarted the armed man?" Burton asked, looking Clint up and down.

"That he did," Gallows said, "and without a shot being fired. Mr. Burton, this is my friend, Clint Adams . . . also known as the Gunsmith."

"The Gunsmith?" Burton frowned a moment, then his face brightened. "Ah, even as far away as London I have heard that name. You are a legend of the old West, eh?"

"Well, not real—"

"That's exactly what he is," Gallows said, cutting Clint off, "and I've just asked him to become Miss Bernhardt's personal bodyguard."

"But . . . I thought that was the position we had retained you to fill, sir?" Burton said.

"I can't be with Miss Bernhardt all the time," Gallows said. "You've also retained me to make arrangements to get her to and from the theater, the hotel, the railway station . . . I just need one other man I can trust to look after her every minute."

"That does make sense, then," Burton agreed. He looked at Clint. "I welcome you, then—"

"Oh, it's not official yet," Clint said.

"Why not?"

"I haven't accepted the job yet."

"Is Mr. Gallows not offering you adequate remuneration?" the Brit asked.

"No, no, he's offered me plenty," Clint said. "But Miss Bernhardt has not okayed my hiring."

"Well, there's no need to worry about that," the man said. "I'll just have a word with her—"

"That's all right, Mr. Burton," Clint said. "I'm going upstairs to meet her in just a few moments. Once she and I have had a talk we'll see if she accepts me, and if I accept the job."

"Excellent!" Burton said. "I'll come up with you."

"I think it would be better if I went up alone, sir," Clint said "if you don't mind."

"Well—"

"In fact," Clint went on, "I think even Jack should stay down here with you. I'll go up and introduce myself. I don't think it will take long for the lady and me to form our opinions of each other."

"And what time is this meeting scheduled to take place?" Burton asked.

"Noon," Clint said.

Gallows took out a pocket watch and said, "Just ten minutes from now."

"Do you think the lady would mind if I was early?" Clint asked them both.

"Not at all," Burton answered. "Punctuality is especially appreciated by Miss Bernhardt, I assure you."

"Good," Clint said. "I'll just go upstairs now and get this job interview over with."

"We'll wait in the bar," Gallows said. "It should be open by noon."

"A drink this early in the day?" Burton said, licking his lips. "A fabulous country, this."

"Yes," Clint said, "I agree."

They all entered the hotel together and in the lobby separated. Clint took the winding staircase to the second floor while Gallows and Burton went to the bar.

SIX

Armed with Sarah Bernhardt's room number Clint made his way down the hall. The local detective Gallows had put on her door at night was gone, but the empty chair was still there, blocking the way. Clint moved the chair aside and knocked on the door.

After a few moments the door opened and the Divine Sarah was standing there, staring at him. Her hair was piled carelessly atop her head, simply to get it out of the way. She was wearing a burgundy dressing gown, cinched tightly at her waist. She was short and slender. Her large eyes regarded him with frank appraisal, which he returned.

"Do you approve of what you see?" she asked.

"Miss Bernhardt," he said, "you are even more lovely in person than you are on stage."

"My goodness," she said, "but you're a charming man for a bodyguard."

"Bodyguards are not supposed to be charming?" he asked.

"Well, I've only met a few," she said, "but that has never been one of the traits I've noticed in them. Even Mr. Gallows is a little—what do you say in this country—rough around the edges?"

"That he is."

"Of course, I'm assuming that you are the man he has hired for the job?"

"Well," Clint said, "he's offered me the job. My acceptance of it is subject to this meeting. My name is Clint Adams."

Her eyes brightened and, for some reason, her very pale skin flushed.

"I know that name, don't I?" she asked.

"Possibly."

"Well, Mr. Adams," she said, "I am Sarah Bernhardt. Please, come in."

She stepped back to allow him to enter and, as he slipped past her, he caught a whiff of her sweet perfume. Closing the door, she turned to face him. Even with minimal attention paid to her face this morning she was beautiful. Although she was in her early forties, she had the complexion of a woman ten years younger. Clint knew that she'd had countless romances with princes and kings over the years, and that she was also rumored to have had relationships with famous authors like Victor Hugo. He could see why men of all ages would fall in love with her, no matter what their status in life was.

"You're staring," she said.

"I apologize," he said, "but I'm sure it's something you're used to . . . from men and women."

"Ah," she said, smiling radiantly, "there's that charm again. I had some coffee brought up. May I offer you some? Or would you prefer something stronger? Brandy, perhaps?"

"Coffee would be fine."

"Please be seated and I will bring it to you."

The suite was lavishly furnished, although Clint was sure it could not compare with some of the accommodations she was used to in Europe. He chose an overstuffed armchair and lowered himself into it. The Colt New Line dug into his lower back and he fidgeted to make a more comfortable adjustment.

She brought over a silver tray with a silver coffeepot and two china cups. She set it down on a nearby table, then poured the two cups full and handed him one. He was struck again at how thin she was, almost ethereal in appearance, and yet there was no indication of frailness. Also, she'd already traveled from Europe to New York and from New York to Cleveland, with stops along the way, and yet she did not seem to be suffering any ill effects.

She took her cup and sat in the armchair's twin, right across from him.

"So, tell me, how long have you been doing bodyguard work, Mr. Adams?" she asked. "Your name is familiar to me, of course, but I did not know this was part of your reputation."

"It's not," he said. "This is not the kind of thing I normally do."

"Oh? Then why do it now?"

"Jack Gallows is a good friend of mine," he said. "He's asked me to help him with this . . . assignment."

"Assignment," she said, digesting the word for a moment. "Well, I suppose I have been called worse."

"I meant no offense."

"And none was taken, I assure you."

"The fact is," he went on, "when I came here I didn't know he was going to ask me to do this."

"You came all this way . . . from where?"

"Texas."

"Without knowing what the job was?"

"That's right."

"But . . . why?"

"I told you," Clint answered. "Jack is my friend. He sent me a telegram saying he needed some help."

"And you came all this way on the basis of that?" she asked. "I'm impressed."

"Don't be," he said. "It's just something one friend does for another."

"And you must be a very good friend to have, Mr. Adams."

"I hope some people think so."

"Oh, I'm sure of it," she said. "Are you acquainted with many people in my profession?"

"That depends on what you're referring to," Clint said. "I know another stage actress, Lillie Langtry."

"Ah, yes, Miss Langtry," Sarah said. "A lovely, talented woman. I saw her perform when she came to London."

"And has she seen you perform?" Clint asked.

"You know, I'm not sure," she said. "Maybe we will run into each other on this tour."

Clint couldn't really tell from the tone of her voice what she thought of Lily, but it was entirely possible she was just being polite.

"And who else?"

"Well, some other folks involved in what I guess you'd call show business," he said. "William Cody is a friend—"

"Ah, the famous Buffalo Bill?" she gushed. "I have seen his show. It's marvelous!"

"Yes. I'm also friends with Annie Oakley."

She set her cup down and clapped her hands together.

"I've also seen her! She's amazing with her pistols."

"Yes, she is."

"Is she as good a shot as you are, Mr. Adams?"

"Probably better."

Sarah stared at him for a few moments, then said, "I think you are being modest."

Rather than reply he said, "And I had the pleasure of meeting P. T. Barnum when I was in New York."

"A fascinating man, I understand," she said. "I haven't met him, myself."

"He is fascinating," Clint said. He didn't bother mentioning that he was now in possession of a horse—his Darley Arabian, Eclipse—that had been given to him as a gift from Barnum.

"Well, then, you've had ample experience with people in my business," she said. "If you agree to be my bodyguard you shouldn't be surprised by anything I might say or do."

"Well, you'll excuse me for saying so, Miss Bernhardt," Clint replied, "but you're a woman, and women always manage to surprise me."

"Mr. Adams," she said, slowly, "I think you and I are going to get along famously . . . just famously!"

SEVEN

Clint found Jack Gallows and John Burton in the hotel bar, seated at a table. Gallows had a beer and Burton what looked like a glass of brandy.

"Clint," Gallows said. "How did it go?"

"It went well," Clint said, "very well."

"Splendid!" Burton said, happily.

"Get yourself a beer," Gallows said. "Make sure they charge it to my room."

Clint went to the bar, and after a nod from Gallows, the bartender drew him a beer on the detective's room. Clint carried it back to the table and sat down. There were only two or three more men sitting in the room, and they were taking no notice of Clint and his party.

"So what's your decision?" Gallows asked. "Will you take the job and help me out?"

"After meeting the lady," Clint said, "how could I say no?"

"That's what I thought would happen," Gallows said.

"Excellent," Burton said. "When will you start?"

"Today," Clint said. "Jack, you'll need to get me a room on her floor."

"No problem," Gallows said. Indicating Burton, he added, "We also have rooms on her floor."

"Then I'll be escorting her to the theater tonight, and I'll remain in the wings while she performs."

"That will not be a problem," Burton said.

"And this is her last performance here?" Clint asked.

"Yes," Gallows said, "we're on to Chicago in the morning."

"I'll need a copy of her itinerary for the remainder of the tour," Clint said.

"I can get that for you, sir," Burton said. "I will have it in your room tonight."

"Thank you. There's just one other thing."

"And what's that?" Burton asked, since Clint was looking at him when he said it.

"I'll be reporting to Jack and only to Jack," Clint said. "You and Miss Bernhardt can have whatever relationship with him you've agreed on, but I'm working for him."

"Well—"

"That shouldn't be a problem, should it, Mr. Burton?" Gallows asked, cutting the little man off.

"Well . . . no, I suppose not," Burton said. "After all, it is your country . . . and we are venturing into a part of the country you are familiar with."

"That's right," Gallows said.

"I have never been to the Wild West, myself," Burton said. "Is it as wild as depicted in Colonel Cody's Wild West Show?"

"Sometimes," Clint said, exchanging a glance with Gallows, "it's even wilder . . ."

Burton was the first to leave, giving Clint a chance to talk with Gallows.

"Who's paying you, Jack?"

"Well, he is," Gallows said. "The money is hers, but he's the one who pays me."

"And you'll be paying me."

"Right."

"I'll need an advance."

"Now?" Gallows asked, reaching into his pocket.

"No, not now," Clint said, "and not here. Later, in my room, before the performance."

"Okay. I'll give you your first week's pay in advance."

"Fine."

Gallows sat forward in his chair.

"So?"

"So what?"

"What did you think?"

"About what?"

"About her, whataya think I'm askin'?"

"Well, she's very impressive."

"I'll say," Gallows said. "Wait until you see the faces of the audience tonight. You'll be able to see it very well from the wings. She holds them in the palm of her hand."

"I noticed that last night."

"And she's a little slip of a thing, but . . . I tell you, it's all I can do not to fall in love with her myself. You better be careful, old friend."

"Don't worry," Clint said. "I'm not about to fall in love. Not after all these years."

Gallows knew that Clint had been close to marriage once, years ago, only to have the woman die violently.

"No, I guess not."

"You haven't gotten married since the last time I saw you, have you, Jack?"

"No," Gallows said, "being married is not good for my business."

"No, I guess not."

Clint finished his beer and pushed the mug away from him.

"I think I'm going to need to buy some new clothes," he said.

"You want to go and do that together now?" Gallows asked.

"I think I can do it myself. Look, about that advance. I will need it now. Why don't you get me a room? I'll move my stuff here from my hotel, and I'll meet you in the room in an hour."

"Sure."

"You can pay me then and I can buy some clothes for tonight and the rest of the tour."

"Okay. Let's go."

"Jack."

Gallows stopped in a crouched position, half-standing and half-sitting.

"What?"

"Is there anything you're not telling me?"

"About what?"

"About this whole bodyguard thing," Clint said.

"Like what?" Gallows straightened and looked down at Clint. "What do you mean?"

"I just don't want you to hold anything back from me," Clint said. "We're not guarding her against anyone in particular, right?"

"Right."

"And that man last night, Bagby. He was after you?"

"It's just like I told you, Clint."

"Okay, then," Clint said. "I just wanted to make sure. After all, you did work for old Allan Pinkerton for a long time, and he usually had his own agenda."

"That was him, Clint," Gallows said, "not me. I'm on the up and up."

"Good," Clint said, standing. "Then I'll see you in my room here in an hour."

EIGHT

The room Jack Gallows secured for Clint Adams was not as lavish as Sarah Bernhardt's, but it was much better than the room he'd had at his hotel. When he returned to the Cleveland House with his belongings, the desk clerk handed him a key and welcomed him as a guest, telling him that all the arrangements had been made through Mr. Gallows.

He was in his room ten minutes when Gallows knocked on his door.

"Here's your first week's pay," he said, handing Clint an envelope. "I've got to go and see about the buggy for to-night and for tomorrow morning."

"Jack, who made all the travel arrangements as far as the trains are concerned?"

"Those were made by Mr. Burton from New York," Gallows told him. "I had nothing to do with those."

"Okay," Clint said. "I'm going to go and find a store to get some theater clothes. If I'm going to be escorting her to theaters across the country I'm going to have to look the part."

"Agreed."

As Gallows was leaving Clint asked, "Is she scheduled for a stop in Denver?"

"Oh, yes," Gallows said. "Three performances there."

"Have you been in touch with Roper?"

"Yep," Gallows said. "Told him when we'd be there and he said he'd make himself available."

"Good," Clint said. "It'll be good to see him when somebody's not shooting at one or the other of us."

"Oh, and one other thing you might find interesting," Gallows said.

"What's that?"

"She's scheduled to do one night, and one night only, at the Birdcage in Tombstone."

"Tombstone?"

"Is that a problem?"

"No," Clint said, "no, it's just been a while since I was there."

"I understand not much has changed since the Earps and the Clantons went at it."

"I guess we'll find that out when we get there," Clint said.

"I guess so."

They left the room together and went down to the lobby. There they split up. Clint went to the front desk and asked the clerk where the nearest store was that carried what he wanted. The man gave him directions to a place that was only a couple of blocks away.

When Clint left the hotel he wore his full-sized Colt in his gun belt, rather than carrying his smaller Colt New Line in his belt.

Two men watched Jack Gallows leave the Cleveland House hotel from across the street and then saw Clint Adams leave.

"Adams is wearin' his gun," one of them said.

"You think he's workin' for Gallows?" the other asked.

"Why else would he be here?" the first man replied. "Why else would he switch hotels?"

"Should we foller them?" the second man asked.

"I think we'd better let the boss know what's goin' on," the first man said, "and see what he wants us to do."

"I think we oughtta foller Adams."

"What for?"

"We might get a chance to take him."

"Are you stupid or what?" the man asked his colleague. "I ain't about to go up against the Gunsmith, just the two of us."

"But the reputation we'd have—"

"Would get us killed, eventually," the first man said. "You want that kind of rep? You take him on yourself."

"Alone?"

"Alone," the first man said. "That'll give you a rep."

The second man thought a moment, then said, "I think we oughtta go see the boss."

"Good thinkin'."

NINE

Clint presented himself at Sarah Bernhardt's door two hours before her performance was to take place. Gallows had informed him that she liked to arrive early. When she opened the door she paused to look him up and down.

"I am impressed," she said. "You clean up very well, Mr. Adams."

"So do you, Miss Bernhardt."

She looked down at her dress and said, "I am hardly dressed for the theater."

"I was talking about last night."

"You were there?"

"Yes, I was."

"Then you've seen me perform before," she said. "I thought tonight would be the first time for you."

"Not far from the truth," he said. "Yesterday was the first time. Are you ready?"

"I just need to collect a few things," she said. "Please come in."

He entered and closed the door behind him.

"Before we get going, maybe we'd better get something straight," he said.

"Like what?"

35

"My name is Clint," he said. "There's no need for you to keep calling me *Mr. Adams*."

"Then you shall have to call me Sarah," she said. "It is only fair, don't you think . . . Clint?"

"Yes, I do, Sarah."

She put some things into a carpetbag, which made it look like she was going on a trip and not just a short ride to the theater.

"I'm ready to go."

He held the door open for her, closed and locked it before they went down to the lobby. Out front, the buggy was already waiting to take them to the theater.

"How have you enjoyed being in this country?" he asked.

"New York was very impressive," she said.

"And the rest of the country?"

"Less impressive the farther west we get, I'm afraid."

"Well, wait until you see the scenery once we get even farther west," he told her. "Then you'll really be impressed."

"I imagine you've spent a lot of time admiring the scenery, haven't you?"

"Oh, yes," he said. "I've spent the majority of my life on the back of a horse. I've seen this country from north to south and from east to west. And I've been to your part of the world."

"Really? What part?"

"London."

He explained to her that he'd gone there for a large gun show but, as with Gallows, he left out the part about the strangler. By the time he was finished with his story they were at the stage entrance to the theater. Apparently, Gallows had already instructed the driver to take the buggy right down the alley to that door.

Clint took Sarah's bag and then helped her down.

"Do you have your instructions for tonight?" he asked the driver.

"Yes, sir," the man said. "Same as last night."

"Okay."

As the man drove away he asked Sarah, "Did you recognize him as the same driver you had last night?"

"Yes, I did."

"Okay, good."

He held the stage door open for her, and then followed her inside to her dressing room. Once there, she turned to face him in the doorway.

"I can take it from here, Clint."

"Just let me come inside for a quick look around," he told her, "and then I'll leave you to get ready."

"You're very thorough," she said, stepping aside to allow him to enter.

He put her bag down on a small divan, then looked around. There were no other doors, and no windows, and no one else was in the room. Also, there was no room for anyone else to get ready. The dressing room was all hers.

"All right," he said, moving to the door, "if you need anything I'll be outside, after I've checked the theater."

"Thank you."

He stepped outside and she closed the door behind him. Before it closed all the way he saw a bemused smile on her face. He wondered if she was of the opinion that she didn't need a bodyguard, and that this was all melodramatic nonsense. Then again, as an actress she probably appreciated melodrama.

Clint walked around the theater, met most of the backstage crew, and then went in search of the theater manager. One of the crew gave him directions to the man's office. He knocked on the door and was surprised when it was flung open almost immediately.

"What the hell is it now?" a mustached man bellowed. When he saw Clint his expression quickly changed from annoyed to sheepish.

"Oh, I'm sorry," he said. "I thought it was another member of my staff with another stupid question."

"Nope," Clint said. "Not a member of your staff, and I hope I don't have a stupid question."

"How can I help you, sir?"

"My name is Clint Adams," he said. "I'm Sarah Bernhardt's bodyguard."

"Bodyguard!" The man looked alarmed. "Has there been a threat?"

"No, no," Clint said, "I've just been hired to look after her for the rest of her tour. I wanted to introduce myself and let you know I'll be backstage for the entire performance."

"Well, that's fine," the man said. "My name is Simms, Ed Simms.

The two men shook hands.

"Tell me, how long is she on stage for?"

"The whole play," he said. "All ninety minutes."

That was good. At least he wouldn't have to keep tabs on her when she was offstage.

"All right, then," Clint said, "I'll be in the wings. Do you have any security men of your own?"

"Just a man on the stage door to keep people from sneaking in," Simms said. "We've never really needed anyone else."

"Okay," Clint said. "Thanks for the information, Mr. Simms."

"I just hope nothing happens," Simms said. "I'd be ruined if something happened to Sarah Bernhardt in my theater."

"Nothing's going to happen, Mr. Simms," Clint said. "I'm here to make sure of that."

TEN

Clint stood outside Sarah Bernhardt's dressing room until moments before curtain, when a young man came to tell Sarah it was time to go on. He looked at Clint nervously, not daring to go near the door.

"It's five minutes to curtain," he said. "I'm, uh, supposed to knock and tell Miss Bernhardt."

"Well, go ahead," Clint said. "I'm not here to stop you from doing your job."

"Yes, sir." He stepped to the door and knocked. "Five minutes, Miss Bernhardt."

"Thank you," she called out.

The young man nodded nervously at Clint, then turned and hurried away.

The door opened and Sarah stepped through. She was as radiant as she had been the night before, when Clint first saw her on stage.

"Wow!" Clint said.

"Do I look all right?" she asked, smoothing down the skirt of her gown.

"That's what *wow* means," he said. "You look wonderful."

"Thank you." She stepped outside and closed the door behind her. "Will you walk me to the stage?"

39

"I'll walk with you and stay in the wings throughout your performance," he promised her.

"Good," she said. "I feel safer, already."

Clint walked with her to the very edge of the stage and stayed quiet while she concentrated.

"I get nervous, you know," she said, sheepishly.

"Really? You? I don't believe it."

"It's true," she said. "I've never gotten used to this part. I'm fine once I'm out there, but this is the part that makes me shake."

"But . . . you're Sarah Bernhardt."

"And you're the Gunsmith," she said. "Are you going to tell me you never get nervous . . . about anything?"

"No," he said, "I can't tell you that."

"Then we're both human," she said.

"Yes," he said, "very human."

The orchestra began to play and she said, "That's my cue."

"Good luck."

"You're supposed to 'say break a leg,' " she told him, "even if you really don't want me to."

"All right, then," he said. "Break a leg."

"Thank you."

She swept out onto the stage and immediately held the audience in the palm of her hand, where they remained for the next ninety minutes.

Jack Gallows was sitting out in the audience, in the first row, keeping his eyes on Sarah and on the crowd. Even he, who had seen her perform countless times now, was amazed at her command on the stage.

From his vantage point he could see Clint standing in the wings, which is where he had been standing for these past few weeks. This was actually the first time he'd seen her perform from the audience and it was all he could do to take his eyes off her to continue to be watchful.

• • •

From where he was standing Clint could see Gallows sitting in the audience. The man seemed intent on Sarah's performance, and several times looked as if he had to drag his eyes from her to watch the audience. Clint wondered how many times Gallows had seen her perform. For his own part, Clint knew that no matter how many times he saw her over the next few weeks he would never get used to her command of the stage and the audience—especially in light of what she had told him about being nervous.

It was very clear why they called her the Divine Sarah.

ELEVEN

After the performance, the applause went on for some time, and when Sarah came offstage she was breathless—and ravenous. She went back to her dressing room, changed her clothes and then she, Clint, Jack Gallows and John Burton went to dinner together at a nearby restaurant which catered to the theater crowd.

As they walked across the floor to a table for six diners, theatergoers sang her praises and even reached out to touch her. At one point a man reached for her and Clint managed to put himself between Sarah and the groping hand.

The manager of the restaurant had two of the six chairs removed so there was plenty of room for the four of them to sit. Clint sat with Sarah on his right, her back to the wall, and Gallows on his left. Burton sat across from him. From his vantage point he could see the entire room.

"How are you feeling, my dear?" Burton asked, his tone extremely solicitous.

"I'm fine, John," she said. "Don't be such a mother hen."

"It's my job to be a mother hen, dear," Burton said. He looked at Gallows and Clint. "This whole tour has been very hard on her, very stressful."

"I'm fine," she said, again. "I'm just a little tired because we have been on the go for so long."

"And how much longer does the tour have to go?" Clint asked.

"Almost a month," Burton said.

"Where do we go from here?" Clint asked. "Jack mentioned Chicago, but what's after that?"

"After Chicago we go to St. Louis," Burton said, "then Kansas City, Oklahoma City . . . mmm, somewhere in Texas . . . in fact, several stops in Texas . . . Fort Worth?"

"And El Paso?" Clint asked.

"Yes! El Paso. How did you know that?"

"Jack mentioned the Birdcage in Tombstone," Clint said. "I just assumed El Paso might be a logical stop just before that."

"I think Phoenix might be after that," Gallows said. "And then several stops in California."

"We end up the tour in San Francisco," Burton said, "and we have a one-week run there."

"And Denver is in there," Gallows reminded them, "somewhere."

"Well," Clint said, "if she's not tired now I bet she'll be tired when the tour is over. What happens after that?"

"Back to England, thank God," Burton said. When he realized all three people at the table were staring at him he added, "No offense to your country, but it will be good to get home where it's—" He stopped himself short.

"Where it's civilized?" Clint asked.

"Well . . ." Burton said.

"Don't mind John," Sarah said. "He is a true Englishman and is not happy anywhere else."

"I can understand that," Clint said.

The waiter came over to take their orders. John Burton ordered something called beef stroganoff, which Clint had heard of but had never had. Clint was surprised when Burton ordered first, not waiting for Sarah to do so, and then was surprised again when he and Gallows deferred to her and she ordered a big steak, rare. He and Gallows then ordered the same thing.

"I'm always starved after a performance," she said.

"You must not eat like this very often," Clint said.

"On the contrary," Burton said. "She's been eating huge steak dinners after her performances since we got to this country. Before long we're going to have to let some of her costumes out."

"John," Sarah said, "I have not gained an ounce since we arrived in America."

"Maybe not . . ." Burton said.

"Looks to me like you could stand to gain a few pounds," Gallows said, and suddenly all eyes were on him. "I'm sorry, I didn't mean to offend . . . I just meant you're so . . . I mean, you're slender, but kinda . . . small . . ." He stopped stammering and looked to Clint for help.

"You're on your own," Clint told him.

"That's all right," Sarah said. "I've taken no offense at what Mr. Gallows has said."

Burton called the waiter back over and ordered a bottle of wine. During dinner, Clint and Gallows ordered a beer each. By the time the steak dinners—and stroganoff—arrived they'd all had a fair amount to drink. Clint was surprised at the amount of liquor Burton was able to hold. His speech never slurred, and his eyes were clear. Sarah's speech did not slur as the level of the wine bottle went down, but he could see in her eyes that she was feeling the effects. She seemed so relaxed that he thought she might nod off.

She perked up, however, when the meal arrived and dug into her steak with gusto. Clint and Gallows did the same, while Burton ate his meal in dainty bites.

Clint listened while the other three told him how the tour had gone to date, and Sarah praised Gallows for being able to head trouble off before it happened.

"I've done okay up to now," Gallows said, "but the farther west we get, the rowdier the audiences are going to get, especially the men."

"And that is why you gave hired Clint?" Sarah said.

"Exactly," Gallows said. "Between the two of us we'll be able to handle anything that comes along."

"I'm very sure of that," Sarah said, pushing her plate away. "Where is our waiter? I'd like to see what they have for dessert."

TWELVE

After dinner they took two buggies back to the hotel, Clint and Sarah in one and Gallows and Burton in the other.

"Your manager seems very concerned about you," Clint said.

"Of course he's concerned for me," she said. "I'm his meal ticket."

"That's kind of a harsh way to look at it."

"It is the only way to look at it," she said. "My relationship with John is purely business."

"Do you have any friends in this country?"

"Not one."

"That's too bad."

"No," she said, "it's not too bad. Not having any friends helps me to focus."

"Must be lonely, though."

She hesitated, then said, "Sometimes it is."

The two buggies pulled up in front of the hotel and the four of them entered the lobby.

"Who's for a nightcap?" Burton asked.

"I could use a drink."

"Mr. Adams?"

47

"I'll join you as soon as I escort Miss Bernhardt to her room," Clint said.

"Good night, gentlemen," Sarah said.

As Clint and the actress went up the stairs, Gallows followed Burton to the bar.

Outside two men were peering in the front door, watching the foursome split up.

"Now what?" the second man asked. His name was Brock.

"Now they're in for the night," the first man, Irons, said. "We have to go and tell the boss."

The two of them turned and walked away from the hotel.

"Can we get a drink first?" Brock asked.

Irons sighed.

"I don't see why not," he said. "He's probably busy right now, anyway."

Frank Long put his hands on the girl's head to slow her down. Her mouth glided wetly over his rigid penis, but he wanted her to go slow. He wasn't in a hurry to finish this. It had taken him a while to find just the right girl, with the correct color of hair and the right body type. She didn't have the accent, and she wasn't as beautiful, but crouched down between Long's legs he could pretend that the girl was Sarah Bernhardt.

And there was another way he could pretend she was Sarah.

"Up!" he said.

She got to her knees between his legs with a smile, rolled over onto her back and spread her legs.

"No," he said. He grabbed her and flipped her over. "Like this. Up on your knees."

She got on all fours and hiked her butt into the air. He got behind her, grabbed her hips, slid his penis up between her thighs and rammed himself into her. He was still ramming her fifteen minutes later when someone knocked on the door.

"Wait," he said to her, withdrawing.

She rolled over onto her back, sweat dripping down her face and took a deep breath.

"No," he said, pointing at her, "stay the other way and wait."

The girl stared at him, then took a deep breath, rolled back over and hiked her skinny butt in the air. She did have lovely skin, though, he thought, as he padded barefoot and naked to the door.

He opened the door and found Brock and Irons standing there. Brock's eyes widened and went immediately to the ass of the girl on the bed and stared.

"What is it?" he asked.

"They had dinner after the show and went back to their hotel," Irons said.

"It was not a show," Long said, "it was a performance. Sarah Bernhardt does not do shows."

"Yes, sir."

"You."

"Yes, sir?" Brock said.

"Stop looking at the girl's ass."

"Yes, sir," Brock said, but his eyes were still on it.

Long took a step and slapped the man in the face. Brock's eyes jerked to him and flared.

"Go ahead," Long said, staring back at him, "go for it."

"Don't," Irons said.

"Shut up, Irons," Long said. "Let your friend make his own decisions."

Brock was many inches taller and about forty pounds heavier than Long, but in the end he backed down. Long could see the light go out in his eyes.

"What do we do now, sir?" Irons asked.

"Go get some sleep," Long said. "In the morning, we're all going to Chicago."

Long slammed the door in their faces and turned his attention back to the naked girl.

"Me, too?" she asked, looking back over her shoulder.

"You, too, what?"

"Am I going to Chicago?"

"No, you stupid cow," he said, getting on the bed behind her.

THIRTEEN

The train ride from Cleveland to Chicago was uneventful. They had four seats together, two facing two, but alternated who sat next to whom. First Burton sat next to Sarah, and, from what Clint could figure, they were going over her performances in Chicago.

"What do you think?" Gallows asked, at one point.

"About what? Sarah?"

"No," Gallows said, "I know what you think of her. What every man thinks of her. I'm talking about Burton."

"What about him? He's her manager."

"He's prissy."

"And?"

"The farther west we go the more out of place he's gonna be," Gallows said. "That might cause trouble."

"That's why we're here, isn't it?" Clint asked. "To handle things when there's trouble, isn't it?"

"Yeah, but we don't need nobody causing trouble, do we?" Gallows asked.

"So talk to him," Clint said. "Educate him on the ways of the West. Keep him from getting us in trouble."

"I can do that, I guess."

"Here, I'll change places with him and you can start."

"Hey, wait—"

Clint got up and stood in front of Burton and Sarah.

"Mr. Burton, Jack would like to talk with you for a little while."

"Oh? Well, we are a little busy—"

"We're done here, John," Sarah said. "Change places with Mr. Adams."

Burton looked at her, then said, "Oh, very well."

He stood up and moved to Clint's seat, and Clint took his place next to Sarah.

"Thank you," she said.

"For what?"

"He was starting to drive me crazy," she said. "He is such a stickler for detail."

"And you're not?"

"Not every minute detail, no," she said. "I know what I have to do when I'm onstage. I don't need to know everything else that's going on. That's John's job."

"And mine and Jack's," he added.

"Yes, right," she said. She had the window seat and looked outside briefly before asking, "So what does Mr. Gallows want to talk to John about?"

"Starting trouble," Clint answered, "or not starting trouble, I should say."

"What?"

Briefly, he explained Gallows's fears that Burton's prissy ways might cause trouble. Clint could see Gallows's point, especially when they got to Texas or to someplace like Tombstone. However, in his explanation he substituted the word *civilized* for *prissy*.

"That's not what Mr. Gallows said," Sarah commented.

"No," Clint said, "I cleaned it up a bit."

"That was very gentlemanly of you," she said. Instead of looking out the window this time, she craned her neck to look at the inside of the railroad car.

"What are you looking for?" he asked.

"Bank robbers," she said. She looked at him earnestly. "Do you think there are any on board?"

"I don't think we have to worry," he said. "Nobody really robs trains, anymore."

"Why not?"

"Banks are easier," he said. "They're not moving." It wasn't necessarily true, but he wanted to put her mind at ease.

"I see." She sat back in her seat. "I suppose I'm rather nervous about going West."

"A lot of what you've read just isn't true," he said. "Other parts are just exaggerated."

"What about you?"

"What about me?"

"Your reputation?" she asked. "Is that exaggerated?"

"Very much so."

"You mean you haven't killed anyone?"

"I've killed men who were trying to kill me," he replied. "I kill to stay alive. That's why most people kill."

"I suppose that's true," she said. "Except for war."

"Men kill in war to stay alive."

"But they start wars for the oddest reasons," she said. "Some of them make no sense. So men end up killing for no good reason."

"Well," he said, "I suppose that's true, too."

"I've never performed in a western theater," she said. "What are they like?"

"Like most theaters," he said. "Some towns don't have a theater, though. Others have theaters like the Birdcage, which is also a saloon and a gambling hall."

"Men gambling and drinking," she said, "are they really interested in seeing a performance?"

"Sarah," he said, "I think I can guarantee they'll be interested in seeing you perform."

FOURTEEN

By the time they arrived in Chicago, Gallows had convinced Burton he wasn't insulting him.

"I thought he was gonna take a poke at me," Gallows said to Clint. They were walking through the train station behind Sarah and Burton, with porters behind them carrying all of Sarah's luggage. Clint and Gallows were carrying their own carpetbags.

"That would have been funny," Clint said. "Did you use the word *prissy*?"

"I did, yeah."

"That was your problem," Clint said. "You're going to have to watch your own language so you don't cause any trouble either, Jack."

"I guess you're right," Gallows said. "These English people sure talk funny. You know they say *shedule* instead of *schedule*?"

"I know," Clint said. "It took some time for me to get used to it when I was there."

"I don't get it," Gallows said. "Why don't folks just talk the same way?"

"We talk different from east to west," Clint pointed out,

"and we talk different from Indians—and they talk different from each other."

"I guess you're right."

When they got outside the station, the porters got them three different cabs, one for Burton and Sarah, one for Clint and Gallows and the last one for all the luggage.

In front of the hotel—a plush place called the Drake—bellmen came out to assist with the luggage. Apparently, all of the hotel employees were aware that Sarah was coming. The four of them were greeted in the lobby by the hotel manager—himself a rather prissy-looking man. Such men did not only come from England, Clint thought.

"It's such a pleasure to have you with us, Miss Bernhardt," he said. "My name is Henry Gates. We have your suite ready for you."

"Thank you."

"And we have another room for your manager."

"We will be needing two more rooms for these gentlemen," she said, indicating Clint and Gallows.

"We can share a room," Clint said.

"Nonsense," Sarah said. "I'm sure Mr. Gates can offer us two more rooms."

"Uh, yes, of course," Gates said. "Would you be needing, uh, suites?"

"Regular rooms would be fine," Gallows said, "but we'll need them on the same floor."

Gates looked at Sarah, who said, "They are my—"

"Security men," Gallows finished for her.

"Yes," she said. "Mr. Jack Gallows and Mr. Clint Adams."

The manager looked at Gallows and nodded, but when he looked at Clint the name suddenly clicked in. Clint could see it on his face.

"Clint . . . Adams?"

"That's right."

Gates looked around, as if looking for someone to tell.

"The Gunsmith?"

"I believe he has been called that," Sarah said.

Henry Gates managed to look excited and frightened at the same time.

"Well . . . well . . ." he stammered, "it's certainly a pleasure to have you with us, as well, uh, sir."

"I'm just part of Miss Bernhardt's staff," Clint said. "If you're going to make a fuss about anyone, make it about her."

"Oh, yes, sir," the manager said, "of course."

"And we'd like to get out of the lobby," Clint added.

"Yes," Gates said. "I'll show you to your rooms, and have your luggage brought up. Just let me arrange for the extra rooms."

They stood in the lobby, Clint and Gallows on the alert, while Gates went to the front desk and came back with keys for all the rooms.

"This is a lovely hotel," she commented.

"And a rather large city," Burton commented. "I think I shall be the most comfortable I've been since we left New York."

"Philadelphia was a large city, John," she commented.

"Perhaps," he said.

"We're ready to go," Gates said, returning to them. "If you'll follow me?"

He took them to an elevator, something Clint had only encountered in New York, and which Gallows had never seen at all.

"We've had the elevator for over a year now," Gates said, as they entered.

"Will it hold all of us?" Gallows asked.

"Oh, certainly," Gates said, "but I will, uh, send it back down for the luggage."

That seemed to mollify Gallows a bit.

"We have these in England," Burton observed, "only we call them lifts."

Jack Gallows looked at Clint, as if to say, "There's that funny talk again." Clint only smiled, and almost laughed at the look on Gallows's face when the elevator lurched into motion and began to ascend.

FIFTEEN

Irons and Brock followed Sarah Bernhardt and her party to the Drake hotel from the train station, leaving Frank Long behind to get himself to his own hotel. They had told their cabdriver to stay back, but not to lose sight of the three-buggy parade ahead of them, which was not very hard to do.

When they reached the Drake, Irons and Brock remained outside, but watched through the front door as the Bernhardt party was greeted by a man they assumed was the hotel manager.

"Can I help you gents with anything?" the doorman asked.

He was a large man in a red uniform, and while Brock and Irons both thought they'd be able to take him easy, they'd been instructed not to start trouble or do anything that would get them noticed.

"No, no," Irons said, "we're just takin' a look inside. Beautiful hotel you have here."

"Yeah," Brock said, "real nice."

"We'll just be moving along," Irons said.

Since Frank Long had been to Chicago before, the two men knew where to find him, so they grabbed a cab from the Drake and went to tell their boss what they'd seen.

•   •   •

Frank Long checked into a hotel several blocks away from the Drake, but the several blocks also put him in an entirely different section of town.

"Mr. Long," the desk clerk said. "Nice to have you back."

"I'd like the same room, please."

"Yes, sir."

There were several hotels around the country that held rooms for Frank Long, just in case he showed up. He had that much money. The Easton was one of those.

"Do you need help with your luggage, sir?"

"Yes," Long said, "and I need another room, for my associates."

"A suite. Sir?"

"Just a regular room," Long said. "Their names are Irons and Brock. They should be along soon." He pointed. "Those are their bags. Have them put in their rooms."

"Yes, sir."

"Those are mine. Have them brought up now."

"Will you be requiring . . . uh, company tonight?"

"Yes, I will," Long said. "I'll need a certain type of woman, so listen carefully . . ."

Clint's room was not a suite, but one room with a bed. That was fine with him. Gallows had the same setup. Sarah had a palatial suite, the best the hotel had to offer, and Burton got a slightly less dramatic two-room suite. He was happy with it until he saw what Sarah had, and then he got a little grumpy about it.

"Anyone hungry?" Clint asked, when they had all taken a look at their rooms.

"I am," Sarah said, "but I want to take advantage of the bathing facilities in my room, first."

"That's fine," Clint said. "We can go downstairs and have a drink while we wait for you."

"Sounds good to me," Gallows said.

"I could do with a good stiff brandy," Burton said.

"Johnny," Gallows said, putting his arm around the smaller man, "we got to get you a real drink."

The conversation on the train seemed to have convinced Gallows that he'd made a new friend. Clint could see by Burton's reaction to Gallows's friendly arm that he didn't quite feel the same way.

"We'll meet you downstairs," Clint told Sarah.

"I'll try not to be too long."

"Take your time," Clint said. "I'm sure you'll be well worth waiting for."

When they got down to the lobby the manager, Gates, came running over to them.

"Is everything satisfactory?"

"Well, as a matter of fa—" Burton started, but Gallows cut him off before he could go any further.

"Everything's fine," he assured Gates.

"Uh, Mr. Adams?"

It suddenly became plain to Clint and Gallows that the man was acting more from fear of Clint than from a desire to help Sarah Bernhardt's party.

"Mr. Gates," Clint said to the man, "I couldn't be happier. Put your mind to rest."

"Oh, well," Gates said, "that's . . . that's wonderful."

"Now we're going to go into your bar and have a drink while we wait for Miss Bernhardt to come down for dinner," Gallows said.

"And will you be dining with us?" the man asked. "We have a marvelous chef and a full wine cellar—"

"We will be dining in your restaurant, yes," Clint said.

"Good," Gates said, clapping his hands together, "then your very first meal in Chicago shall be on me."

"That's fine," Gallows said. "Thanks very much."

Clint and Gallows hurried Burton away to the bar before he could get in a word about his room.

SIXTEEN

As Sarah Bernhardt entered the dining room, Clint saw that telling her she'd be worth waiting for had been an understatement. Although she was not dressed for the stage, she still put every other woman in the room to shame. Her hair, newly washed, gleamed. It was almost as if there was a spotlight on her as she crossed the room.

"Gentlemen," she said, as they rose to their feet.

"Please," Clint said, "sit here."

They'd managed to get what Clint thought of as a secure table, in a corner away from many of the others.

"In the corner?" she asked. "Where it's safe?"

"Yes."

"I suppose I'll have to get used to this," she said, sliding in to sit down.

"It's for your own good, ma'am," Gallows said, as the men reseated themselves.

"You gentlemen must be a drink or two ahead of me," she said.

Clint raised his hand and a young waiter came running over.

"Can I get a drink for Miss Bernhardt?" he asked. His voice shook he was so nervous.

"What a charming young man," Sarah said, which also made him blush. "Yes, I would like a glass of white wine."

"Comin' up, ma'am."

"Bring three more beers for the rest of us," Gallows said.

"And some more of this fine whiskey," Burton said, holding up a shot glass.

"Just the beers, thanks," Clint said.

Gallows turned to Burton.

"We wanted to introduce you to some real whiskey, Johnny," he said, "but I think you've had enough."

"Do you think that I do not know my own limits?" the man asked, grumpily.

"Nobody knows their own limits when they've just been introduced to a new drink," Gallows said, "but don't worry, buddy." He slapped Burton on the back. "We're here to look out for you."

Burton made a rude sound with his mouth and set the empty shot glass down.

"What's wrong with him?" Sarah asked.

"He's drunk," Clint said.

"I've never seen him drunk before," she said, peering at him, intensely.

"From only two drinks," Clint added.

"And you called him . . . Johnny?" she asked Gallows. "No one has ever called him that."

"He told me I could," Gallows said, with a shrug.

"After the second drink," Clint added.

"He'll be okay after he has some food," Gallows said.

"We ordered four steak dinners," Clint told her. "I hope you don't mind."

"I don't mind," she said, "but . . . John doesn't eat steak."

"He does now," Gallows said.

"After," Clint said, "the second drink."

The waiter returned with all the drinks. When he set

them down Burton immediately grabbed his and drank half of it.

"We're gonna be needing that food real soon," Gallows said to the waiter.

"It's coming up, sir."

Sarah picked up her wine and sipped it.

"This should be fun," she said.

Clint and Gallows finished their steak dinners first, followed by Sarah. When they were done they sat back and watched Burton demolish his in methodical fashion.

When he was done he set down his knife and fork, sat back and touched his stomach with both hands.

"I can see now why you like this meal, Sarah," he said. "I feel quite . . . content."

Sarah leaned over to Clint, who also leaned over to lend his ear.

"He is going to regret all of this in the morning, isn't he?" she asked him.

"Who knows?" Clint said. "Maybe not."

They both looked at him and watched as he drained his beer mug again.

"Are you going to need him tomorrow for anything?" Clint asked. "I mean, tomorrow morning?"

"I need to go to the theater, meet with the manager and the crew," she said, "but you and I could do that."

"Yes," Clint said, "I suppose we could."

"Waiter," Burton called out. "Another beer."

Gallows looked at Clint, who shrugged and nodded, then turned to Sarah and said, "And I guess we will."

SEVENTEEN

Later, after Sarah had gone back to her room, and after John Burton had been put to bed in his, Clint and Gallows went back to the bar for a last beer of the night. That was when Clint said to Gallows, "We were followed from the train station."

"I know," Gallows said. "I saw. Two men."

"Did you recognize them?"

"I didn't get a good look at their faces."

"Maybe they were simply also coming to this particular hotel," Clint suggested.

"They didn't come in," Gallows said. "And I checked with the desk clerk. No one checked in after us."

Clint was impressed that Gallows had already checked with the front desk.

"So what do we do?" Clint asked.

"Keep our eyes open," Gallows said. "If we see them again we'll have to make a point of meeting them."

"Maybe they're just overanxious fans of hers," Clint said. "Maybe they recognized her at the train station and wanted to see where she was staying."

"Yeah," Gallows said, "maybe."

They finished their beers and walked out to the lobby together.

"You tired?" Gallows asked.

"Not particularly."

"I'm gonna check with the desk again, see if anyone else has checked in, then I'm gonna ask about other ways in and out. Why don't you check the front, have a talk with the doorman?"

"Good idea. I'll meet you back here."

Gallows nodded and they went their separate ways.

Clint stepped outside, took a deep breath and then looked up and down the street, as well as directly across it. Satisfied that no one was watching the hotel, he turned his attention to the doorman.

"Were you on duty when I arrived with Sarah Bernhardt?" he asked the doorman. He was a big, hulking man who looked as if his shoulders were going to burst the seams of his jacket.

"Indeed, I was, sir," the man said. "I made a point of it. I ain't gonna get a chance to see her in the theater, so I wanted to make sure I saw her arrive."

"You don't have time to go to the theater?"

"I got the time," he said, "but on my salary I ain't about to be able to afford tickets for me and the misses."

"After we arrived," Clint said, "did anyone else enter the hotel lobby behind us?"

"No, sir," the man said. "Not for at least an hour."

"Okay, thanks."

"Sir?" the man said, as Clint started to go back inside.

"Yes?"

"There were two men who arrived right after you," the man said.

"But you just told me there wasn—"

"You asked me if they went in," the doorman said. "They didn't go in. They stood out here, peering into the lobby. At the time I thought they were just trying to get a look at Miss Bernhardt."

"Maybe they were," Clint said. "What did they look like?"

"Ruffians," the man said. "Not the type of men who would stay here at all."

"Did you speak with them?"

"I approached them to see what their business was," he said. "I was going to have them move on, but they moved of their own accord. Said they were just curious about the hotel."

"I see," Clint said. He thought a moment, then asked, "What's your name?"

"Jerry, sir."

"Jerry what?"

"Jerry Cable."

"Well, Jerry, I'd like you to do something for me," Clint said. "If you see those men again, I want you to let me know right away. Send a message to my room to see if I'm there. If I'm not, then see if I'm in the bar or leave a message at the desk. Can you do that?"

"Of course, sir."

"And in return," Clint said, "I'll leave tickets for you and your wife at the box office for whatever night you say."

"Really?" The man lost all vestige of his businesslike demeanor. "You'd do that?"

"Sure, I'll do it."

"Wow, my wife is gonna be so excited. Would tomorrow night be okay? I'm off."

"That's fine," Clint said, "but pass this on to whoever replaces you, and also to the other doormen on the staff."

"I'll let them know, sir," Jerry said. "Any suspicious characters hanging around the hotel, and we'll let you know."

"Okay, Jerry." He put out his hand. "My name is Clint Adams."

"Clint . . . Adams?" the man asked, taking Clint's hand by reflex.

"That's right," Clint said, "but keep that under you hat, too, will you?"

"Uh, sure, Mr. Adams," Jerry said, "sure I will. Jeez, Sarah Bernhardt and the Gunsmith staying here at the same time. Can I tell my wife?"

"You can tell her, but make sure she knows not to tell anyone else, okay?"

"Yes, sir."

"Thanks, Jerry," Clint said. "Thanks a lot."

EIGHTEEN

Clint met up with Gallows in the lobby and told him about his conversation with the doorman.

"Okay," the detective said. "I checked with the desk clerk and no one checked in after us."

"What about other entrances and exits?"

"There are several, and I think we'd better check them out."

"Let's split them up," Clint suggested.

"No," Gallows said, "I think you should go to your room. One of us should be on the same floor with her. I'll go and take a look at the other doors, so we know where they are."

"I should back you up."

"I don't think anything is gonna happen tonight," Gallows said. "Besides, I'm just gonna locate the doors and make sure they stay locked at all times."

"Okay," Clint said, "but knock on my door before you go to your room so I know you're okay."

"Yes, Dad."

"Hey," Clint said, "this is what you hired me for, remember?"

"I hired you to watch out for Miss Bernhardt, not me."

71

"Comes with the job," Clint said. "Package deal."

Gallows said, "Okay, I'll knock."

Once again they split up, Clint going up to his room, and Gallows going off into the bowels of the hotel.

Clint entered his room and went immediately to the window. He knew that all their rooms overlooked the street above the front entrance. However, there were no rooftops or ledges outside the rooms, so there was no access from there. If anyone wanted to get into the rooms they'd have to come through the door.

He decided to walk down the hall and listen at Sarah's door, just to be on the safe side. He also figured he'd do the same thing at the manager's door.

In the hall, he stopped first at Burton's door and pressed his ear to it. He could hear, very clearly, that the man was snoring. Next, he moved to Sarah's door and listened, but heard nothing. She had a suite, though, and was probably in the bedroom. He wondered if she'd had time to get dressed for bed and fall asleep since she'd left them, and he decided that she had. He didn't want to wake her, so he started back down the hall to his own room. At that moment, the door to Sarah's room opened and she stuck her head out.

"I thought I heard someone out here."

"I'm sorry," he said. "I didn't mean to disturb you."

"No, that's all right," she said. "I couldn't sleep, anyway. Would you, uh, come in for a moment, Clint?"

"Sure." He turned and walked back to her door. She backed up and allowed him to enter, and he closed the door behind himself.

"Are you all right?" he asked.

She hugged her arms, as if chilled.

"I'm fine, physically," she said.

"Physically?"

"I just mean I'm not that tired yet," she said. "Could we talk awhile?"

"Sure," he said.

"Let's sit."

She sat on the plush divan in the center of the room, and he chose an equally comfortable armchair.

"I had the feeling tonight that you and Mr. Gallows were . . . preoccupied."

"Oh? About what?"

"I thought you would tell me," she said. "I mean, I thought we all had great fun . . . at John's expense . . . but still, there seemed to be something on your mind. Can you tell me, honestly?"

"Well, we compared notes later," Clint said, "and Jack and I both thought we might have been followed from the train station."

"By whom?"

"Two men," he said, "but they just might have been fans. The doorman said two men were trying to look into the lobby to catch a glimpse of you."

Now she looked preoccupied.

"That happens, doesn't it?" he asked. "All the time?"

"I suppose so."

"Oh, come on," he said. "Men are always trying to catch sight of you."

"In Europe, where I'm known, yes," she said. "But not here."

"I think you're better known here than you think," he said.

"That's nice of you to say," she replied. "So you really don't think we have anything to worry about?"

"Not yet," he said. "I'll let you know when we do."

"I can count on you, can't I, Clint?"

He got up from his chair and moved to the sofa, took her hand.

"Of course you can, Sarah," he said. "I'll keep you safe, and tell you the truth at all times."

She smiled then, a smile that lit up the room, and said, "That will make you a very rare man, indeed."

For a moment Clint thought she was going to kiss him, and he knew he would kiss her back, but a knock on the door kept him from finding out for sure.

NINETEEN

Frank Long got off the bed when there was a knock at his door. It was either his two men or the whore. He knew which he preferred, but when he opened the door it was Irons and Brock.

"You boys know where your room is?" he asked.

"Uh, yes, sir," Irons said.

"Brock, you go to your room. Irons will be along in a minute."

"Uh, okay, sure."

As Brock walked back down the hall, Long looked expectantly at Irons.

"They went to the Drake hotel, sir."

"Did you see them go in?"

"Yes, sir."

"Okay, then. Get some sleep and be out in front of that hotel early in the morning."

"Yes, sir."

"And Irons."

"Sir?"

"Don't be seen."

"No, sir. We'll try not to be."

"No," Long said, "you don't understand. I didn't mean try not to be seen. I meant . . . do not be seen. Understand?"

"Uh, yes, sir. I understand. We won't be seen."

"See that you're not."

He closed the door even before Irons had turned to walk away. About five minutes later there was another knock on his door. This time, it was the whore.

Clint got up from the divan and answered the door with his hand on his gun. He cracked the door and saw Gallows standing in the hall.

"Thought you might be in here when you didn't answer your door," Gallows said. "Can we talk in the hall?"

"You might as well come in," Clint said. "I've already told Sarah about the possibility of being followed."

Gallows lowered his voice and asked, "Do you think that was wise?"

"She appreciates honesty, Jack," Clint said. "I think that's what we should give her."

He swung the door wide open and Gallows nodded and stepped into the suite.

"Mr. Gallows."

"Miss Bernhardt," he said, with a slight bow that looked awkward to Clint.

"Is everything all right?"

"Yes, ma'am," Gallows said. "I was just checking in before turning in for the night."

"What about the other doors to the hotel?" Clint asked.

Gallows turned to Clint and said, "They're all secure. The only one that might be a problem is the door to the kitchen, and that'd be during the day."

"Okay," Clint said. "Then I guess we can all go to bed."

Both men turned to Sarah.

"Yes," she said, "I suppose it is time. I don't want to have lines on my face tomorrow."

"And lovely lines they'd be," Clint said. "Come on, Jack."

Sarah walked them to the door and said, "Good night, gentlemen," before closing it.

Gallows's room was in the same direction as Clint's, so they walked down the hall together. When they passed Burton's door Gallows pointed to it and raised his eyebrows.

"Go ahead and listen," Clint said.

Gallows put his ear to the door, then moved away, grinning.

"Sawing some serious wood," he said.

"I don't know if he's going to be feeling too friendly toward us tomorrow," Clint said, as they reached his door.

"Ah, Johnny'll be okay."

"Yeah, well, I don't know if I'd try calling him Johnny tomorrow," Clint said.

"Good night, Clint."

"'Night, Jack."

Clint remained in his doorway until he saw Gallows enter his room with a wave, and then he went inside himself.

TWENTY

Frank Long woke up the following morning next to the whore. She was lying naked on her back, her little breasts almost disappearing. But it wasn't breasts Long was interested in. This whore was the closest he'd come yet to Sarah Bernhardt's skin. It was smooth and pale, like that of the actress. When he had the whore's face buried in a pillow, and her little ass in the air, he could almost imagine it was Sarah Bernhardt. The only problem was when this one spoke. She had a horrible accent and a high-pitched voice. In the middle of the night he offered her extra money if she wouldn't speak.

"It's yore money," she said, with an unconcerned shrug.

Now he reached out and ran his hand over her breasts and her belly, then slid it farther down so he could dig his fingers through her pubic hair. He had no idea if Sarah Bernhardt would look like that down there. The girl moaned and crossed her legs. He lifted his fingers to his nose. He had no idea if the actress would smell this way.

He touched the whore again, and she squirmed.

"Whataya doin'?" she cried out. "It's early!"

He knew one thing, though. Sarah Bernhardt would never sound like that.

His lifted his foot and kicked the whore out of bed.

• • •

Clint woke and couldn't remember if any plans had been made for breakfast. He washed himself, using the hotel's modern facilities, but decided to put a full bath off until another day. The hotel had supplied several different types of cologne, and he slapped one on, being careful not to overdo it. You didn't see this kind of thing in the West, and you certainly never wore cologne, or you'd never hear the end of it.

He got dressed and paused over his gun belt. If he tried to walk around the streets of Chicago with it strapped on he was sure to be approached by some policeman. He pulled the Colt New Line out of his carpetbag and stuffed it into his belt at the small of his back. Then he stood in front of the mirror for a moment, removed the small gun and took his larger Colt out from his holster. He shoved the full-sized gun into his belt. It was no more or less uncomfortable at the small of his back than the smaller gun had been. He grabbed a jacket and put it on, then turned to look at his back. Couldn't see the bulge of the gun. He decided to go with the larger weapon, if only because there was a possibility someone had followed them from the train station.

He assumed that the actress would rise early, so he left his room and walked down the hall to hers.

Sarah Bernhardt answered the door fully dressed, wearing a blouse, a long skirt and shoes with a lot of buttons on them. She asked him to come in.

"Do you have a telephone in your room?" she inquired.

"No."

"I do," she said. "Apparently I can call downstairs for coffee or food. Shall I do that?"

"Coffee would be good," Clint said. "I assume when Jack and Mr. Burton wake up they'll come here. Might as well have them bring four cups."

So she ordered coffee, and they made small talk until it

arrived. She poured him a cup, handed it to him, then poured one for herself and sat down. She was on the divan, he on the armchair.

That was when she said, "We had a moment last night."

"A moment?" he asked.

"You know what I mean," she said. "Last night, when we were on the divan and Mr. Gallows knocked on the door. He interrupted us. We had . . . a moment. You felt it, too."

"Sarah," he said, "we were both tired, and you were frightened. . . ."

"I know what I felt, Clint," she said. "If Mr. Gallows hadn't knocked on the door—"

She stopped when there was a knock on the door.

"See?" she said.

Clint laughed, got up and went to the door. He expected to see Gallows, but instead it was John Burton.

"Oh, my God," Burton said, staggering into the room. "What did we do last night?"

"Good morning, John," Sarah said. "Would you like to have some coffee?"

"I demand to have some coffee."

He continued to stagger until he got to the chair Clint had vacated and dropped into it. Sarah handed him a cup of coffee on a saucer, and it rattled as he took it.

Clint closed the door, wondering when Gallows would happen along.

Burton slurped the coffee, then held his head and said, "Someone tell me what happened last night."

"I think you and Jack went drinking, Johnny," Clint said.

"Drinking?" Burton said.

"That's right."

"Jack?" He looked at Sarah.

"Mr. Gallows."

Then he looked at Clint and repeated, "Johnny?"

"I'll let Jack explain it to you when he gets here."

TWENTY-ONE

When Gallows showed up at Sarah's door they told him he was baby-sitting John Burton.

"Baby-sitting?"

"Yes," Sarah said. "He needs some care."

"Johnny is your friend," Clint reminded him.

"Jesus," Gallows said.

"There's still some coffee left," Clint said. "Sarah and I are going to have breakfast, and then I'll take her over to the theater."

"We'll catch up with you there," Gallows said.

In his chair, John Burton let out a groan and put his head in both of his hands.

"Or maybe we'll still be here," Gallows added.

Sarah touched Gallows on the arm and said, "Take good care of him."

"Yes, ma'am."

"And don't give him any more to drink," Clint added.

"Hair of the dog, you know," Gallows said.

"Up to you," Clint said. He opened the door for Sarah and followed her out.

• • •

Over breakfast Sarah asked Clint, "Can we talk about our moment now?"

"We did have a moment, Sarah," Clint agreed, "but to do anything more about it would be . . . awkward."

"Why?"

"Well, for one thing you're Sarah Bernhardt."

She sat back in her chair.

"What's that got to do with anything?"

"Well, I would think that your country would want you to be above reproach when visiting another country."

"Bollocks," she said.

"What?"

"Um, you would say . . . balls?"

"Oh."

"Who I am—or who you are, for that matter—shouldn't make a difference. What's your other excuse?"

"Well . . . technically, I'm working for you."

"No," she said, "Mr. Gallows is working for me. You're working for him. Any more excuses?"

"Um . . ."

"Do you not find me attractive?" she asked.

"You know that's not true," he said. "You're beautiful."

"Are you married?"

"No."

"Is there someone special?"

"No."

"Then it seems to me that takes care of all the potential problems," she said.

He sat back in his chair now and said, "Well . . . I guess."

"Then we should discuss this at another time," she said, "when we are alone."

And with that she sat forward and continued to eat her breakfast.

•   •   •

When they reached the front door of the hotel Clint stopped her and said, "Wait here."

"Yes, sir."

He went outside and engaged the doorman.

"My name is Clint Adams."

"Yes, sir," the man said. "I'm Phillip. Jerry told me what you wanted, sir, and I haven't seen anybody hanging around."

"That's good," Clint said. "Thanks to you and Jerry. Can you get us a cab?"

"Yes, sir."

The doorman went to the street and Clint stood where he was and looked up, down and across the street. If there was anyone watching them they were well hidden.

"I've got a driver for you, sir," Phillip said, returning.

"Thanks. I'll be right out."

He went back inside.

"Is everything all right?" Sarah asked.

"It looks to be," he said. "We're going to walk outside and get into a cab, but Sarah . . ."

"Yes?"

"It's important that you do what I tell you when I tell you, without question. Is that clear?"

"Yes, it is."

"Good. Let's go, then."

He took her arm and ushered her outside and walked her to the cab where the doorman was waiting. It was he who assisted her into the back of the cab. Clint slipped the man some money, then got into the cab with her. He leaned forward so he could tap the driver on the shoulder.

"We're going to the . . ." He stopped and looked at Sarah.

"The Orpheum."

"The Orpheum Theater," he repeated to the driver.

"Yes, sir."

As they pulled away he looked behind them to see if any cabs or buggies were following, but there were none.

"All right?" she asked.

He sat back, pressed his shoulder to hers and said, "All right."

For now.

TWENTY-TWO

The Orpheum was a much larger theater than the one in Cleveland. That presented more problems for security. There were so many doors in and out that Clint felt the only way he could truly protect Sarah was to stay with her at all times. To this end, they went to meet the theater manager together.

His name was Hector Tierney. In his fifties and on the portly side, he was very excited to have Sarah Bernhardt in his theater.

"And I'm pleased to meet you . . ." he said to Clint, putting his hand out.

Clint decided not to give the man his full name and shook the man's hand, introducing himself simply by his first name.

"And you are . . ."

"Miss Bernhardt's security man."

"Ah." Tierney looked at Sarah. "I was expecting to meet your manager, Mr. Burton?"

"He will be along later," she assured him. "I'm here to see my dressing room and look at the theater."

"I'll be happy to show you around personally," Tierney said, and he proceeded to do so.

He walked alongside Sarah the whole time, with Clint falling in behind them. Sarah was satisfied with her dressing room and with the stage itself. Tierney kept asking her if there was anything else he could do, anything she wanted in her dressing room, but she told him that everything was fine. She made no demands of him, which he didn't seem to understand.

When she was completely satisfied, Clint took over and asked the man about exits and entrances. He also asked about the theater's own security and he was told that they usually had a man watching the stage door, just like the theater in Cleveland. This was when Clint decided that he would stay with Sarah the entire time.

Clint decided that he and Sarah should sit in her dressing room and talk, so they told the manager, Tierney, that they really didn't want to take up any more of his time. He didn't seem to want to leave them alone, but in the end they persuaded him to leave them.

"What do you think?" he asked.

"The theater is fine," she said. "It's not . . . amazing, but it's fine, good enough for two performances."

"And this dressing room?"

She looked around. It was small and cramped, but she said, "It'll do."

"I'm going to stay with you the whole time tonight, Sarah," he said. "I think it's better that way."

"The whole time?"

"Well," he said, "while you're dressing I'll be standing outside, but other than that, yes, the whole time. There are just too many ways in and out of this building."

"That'll be good, Clint," she said. "I'll feel safer that way."

"Jack will be prowling around, too," he said. "Everything will be okay."

"Do you think we could see some of the city now?" she asked.

"You mean . . . this afternoon?"

"Yes," she said. "Let's go right from here. I would like to see the sights and perhaps Lake Michigan. I am more excited about Chicago than I was about Cleveland."

"Well," he said, "I can't say I blame you for that. Should we check in with Jack and Burton?"

She was sitting at what would be her dressing table, and he was seated opposite her. She leaned forward and put her hand on his knee.

"Can't we just play hooky for the afternoon?" she asked. "We can go back to the hotel for dinner."

"If you really want to do that, okay, we'll do it," he said. "I asked the cabdriver to wait outside. Maybe we can get him as a driver—and a guide—for the entire afternoon."

"That would be marvelous."

"Well," he said, "let's go out and ask him."

Irons and Brock had received new instructions from Frank Long that morning.

"They'll have to go to the theater to check it out," he told them. "Instead of watching the hotel, go to the theater and wait for them to show up. Also, get the lay of the place for me."

Now they were across the street from the theater. They had arrived earlier than Sarah Bernhardt and her man, taken a look around the place, and then found a position across the street.

"What's he gonna do?" Brock asked.

"Who?"

"Long," Brock said. "The boss. What's he gonna end up doin' about this actress?"

"I don't know," Irons said. "I ain't asked him that. We're just supposed to do what he pays us to do."

"All the whores he gets look just like her," Brock said. "Did you notice that?"

"No, I didn't," Irons said. "I don't care about no whores. I only care about the money he pays us."

"I'm just sayin' I noticed, is all," Brock said. "They looked like her."

"So what?"

"So, I think he wants her," Brock said. "I'm wonderin' if he's gonna ask us to snatch her."

"If he pays me enough," Irons said, "I'll snatch her, and I'll hold her down while he fucks her."

"You think he wants to do that?"

Irons gave Brock an annoyed look.

"Didn't I just tell you I don't care?"

Brock shrugged and said, "I'm just talkin'."

"Well, do me a favor and stop talkin', will ya?" Irons asked. "He ain't payin' me enough to listen to you yap all day long."

"I'm just tellin' ya—"

"Shut up!" Irons said. "There they are."

The two men watched as Sarah Bernhardt came out with her bodyguard and approached the cab they'd come in. They had a long conversation, and then the man gave the cabdriver some money and helped the actress inside.

"Quick," Irons said. "Go get us a cab."

"Where?"

"On the street, damn it!" Irons said. "And hurry up. They're drivin' away . . ."

TWENTY-THREE

Breakfast seemed to do a lot to cure John Burton's headache. It did a lot to stop the rumbling in Jack Gallows's stomach, too.

"What did I drink last night?" Burton asked.

"Whiskey," Gallows said, "and lots of it."

"And I woke up with a terrible taste in my mouth," the smaller man said. "What did I eat?"

"Steak."

"I ate steak?"

"And you loved it."

Burton looked surprised.

"I don't remember any of it."

"Well," Gallows said, "maybe we'll just let you go back to drinkin' what you want to drink, and eatin' what you want to eat."

"That might be a good idea," Burton agreed. "Right now I would like more coffee."

Gallows waved and the waiter came over and agreed to bring them another pot.

"Where is Sarah?" Burton asked then.

"She and Clint went to the theater."

"I should have gone with her."

"She's with Clint." Gallows said. "She'll be all right. Johnny, there's somethin' I got to ask you."

"Please . . ." the other man said, raising his hand.

"What?"

"My name is John," Burton said.

"All right," Gallows agreed, "somethin' else we'll go back to. Anyway, I got to ask you a question."

"Ask what you like."

"Do you know of anyone who might be . . . followin' Sarah?"

"Following her?" Burton asked. "You mean . . . all the way from England?"

Briefly, Gallows told Burton about his and Clint's belief that someone had followed them from the train station.

"So, we don't know if they followed her from England, from New York, from Cleveland, or just from the station," he finished. "That's why I'm askin' you."

"She has ardent fans in England," Burton said, "royalty, in fact. The King of—"

"Would any of them follow her here?"

"Perhaps," Burton said, "but if they did, they would have let her know they were here. I can't think of anyone who would follow her . . . surreptitiously."

"Surrep . . . what?"

"Secretly."

"Oh," Gallows said. "I see. Okay, then do you know anyone who's got it in for her?"

"Got it in . . . ?"

"Anyone who wants to hurt her," Gallows said. "Any . . . competitors? Has she been threatened?"

"Who in the world would want to threaten her?" Burton asked. "She is an angel."

"I'm sure she is," Gallows said, "but not everybody likes angels, you know."

"It's . . . ridiculous," Burton said. "Absurd."

"Okay, okay," Gallows said, as the waiter returned with the fresh coffee, "I'm just askin'."

"We don't have time for more coffee," Burton said, standing abruptly. "We must go to the theater. I must be with Sarah."

"Okay," Gallows said. "Let's go."

He apologized to the waiter, told him to charge the meal to Burton's room and then tipped him generously. By this time Burton had made it out to the lobby and Gallows had to run to catch up to him.

TWENTY-FOUR

"What do you mean you lost them?"

Frank Long did not raise his voice, but it was clear to Irons that the man was angry. Brock simply sat next to Irons, across from Long, and remained silent. This was by agreement with Irons, who knew that Long did not like the other man.

"They came out of the theater," Irons explained, "jumped into a cab and took off. We tried to get a cab to follow them, but one didn't come along."

Long paused over his steak breakfast. They were at a restaurant around the corner from his hotel, where he usually ate when he was in town.

"You should have planned ahead," he said, "had a cab waiting for you."

"Yes, sir."

"Irons, I don't want to have to tell you how to do everything," Long said.

Long still hadn't raised his voice, but they were attracting the attention of the other diners, anyway.

"And now I suppose you want me to tell you what to do next?" Long asked.

Irons didn't answer. Long took the time to chew a large piece of steak, then sighed and sat back in his chair.

"This is what I want you to do . . ."

When Gallows and Burton arrived at the theater and introduced themselves to the manager, Burton became agitated that Sarah Bernhardt was not there.

"Where did she go?" Burton asked Tierney.

"Well, I really don't know," the theater manager said. "I believe she left with the fellow she was with . . . her security man?"

"Clint," Gallows said.

"That was him," the manager said. "He does work for her, doesn't he?"

"Yes," Gallows said. "He does. Thanks a lot."

"Do you want to go over the theater?" Tierney asked.

Gallows looked at Burton and said, "We might as well, since we're here."

Burton, still annoyed, said, "Very well."

"I'll show you around . . ." Tierney said.

The cabdriver was only too happy to take their money and show the sights to Sarah Bernhardt. He had no idea who she was, but the money was good. After driving them around for a couple of hours he took them down by Lake Michigan, so they could walk by the water.

"This has been very relaxing," Sarah said to Clint.

"I guess you needed to relax," he said. "Whose idea was this tour anyway?"

"I have to admit John talked me into it," she said. "He felt I was ready for a tour of America."

"Well, from the way I've seen the audiences react, I can't say he was wrong."

"Yes, they have been very kind to me."

"Kind?" Clint asked. "I think they've simply recognized your talents and your beauty. There's nothing kind about that, Sarah. You're getting what you deserve."

She turned to him and said, "Now you're being kind."

"Sarah," he said, and suddenly she was in his arms and he was kissing her. Her lips were soft, her mouth hot and avid. He put his arms around her and held her close, their bodies mashed together.

When they broke the kiss, she was gasping for hair, her eyes wide and glassy.

"Here's that moment again," she said.

"And here we are in a place where we can't take advantage of it."

"Time to go back to the hotel," she said. "I still have some time before I have to get ready."

"Sarah—"

She pressed her forefinger to his lips and said, "Before you asked me if I think it's a good idea, and the answer is definitely yes."

He kissed her again, shorter this time, and said, "I think so, too, but what's your manager going to think?"

"What he doesn't know won't hurt him," she said.

They walked back to the buggy and Clint told the driver to take them back to the hotel.

When they approached the front door of the hotel, both of them were excited about getting to her room. The doorman came up to them and Clint noticed that it was Jerry, back on duty again.

"Mr. Adams."

"Oh, hello, Jerry."

"Miss Bernhardt." The doorman tipped his hat and then turned to Clint. "Can I talk to you, sir?"

"Sure, Jerry," Clint said. "Sarah, why don't you wait in the lobby?"

"All right."

When she had gone inside Clint asked, "What is it, Jerry?"

"Those two men you were asking about?"

"Yes."

"They're back."

Clint stiffened.

"Where are they?"

"Right at this moment," Jerry said, "they're across the street watching us, sir."

TWENTY-FIVE

Clint went into the lobby and told Sarah she should go to her room.

"Alone?"

"For the moment," he said. "I have to go across the street."

"For what?"

He hesitated, then decided to go ahead and tell her.

"There are two men across the street watching the hotel?" she asked.

"That's right."

"And they're probably armed?"

"I would think so."

"And you're going over there alone?"

"I have to find out what they want."

"But alone?" she asked. "Do you even have a gun?"

"Of course."

"But . . . it will be two against one."

"I'll try to be gentle with them," he promised.

"Clint—"

"Come on," he said, "I'll walk you to your room."

"Good," she said, grabbing his left arm. "Maybe I can talk you out of it."

"I doubt it."

"Or maybe Mr. Gallows will get back."

"That might happen."

"In fact," she said, as they got into the elevator, "maybe he's in his room."

"We might as well check," he said. "We have to go by it, anyway."

Gallows was not in his room, and neither was Burton—not that he would have been any help.

When Clint got Sarah to her door, he opened it with her key and shoved her inside.

"Close the door and lock it."

"But—"

"Sarah, remember when I told you that you'd have to do what I say when I say it?"

"Yes, but—"

"And you agreed?"

"Yes—"

"Well," Clint said, "it's time." And he pulled the door closed behind him.

Inside the room Sarah paced nervously, then realized that her window overlooked the front of the hotel. She rushed to the window and waited for Clint to appear.

Clint got to the lobby and checked in with the doorman again.

"Are they still there, Jerry?"

"Yes, sir. They're in the doorway to that redbrick building. See it? It's in the shadows."

"I see it."

"If you walk to the end of the street and cross there you could probably sneak up on them."

"If they don't follow me . . ."

"Sir, if I could . . ."

"Go ahead."

"Aren't you afraid that they're following Miss Bern-hardt?" Jerry asked. "If you leave the hotel without her, perhaps they won't follow you at all."

"You have a good point, Jerry," Clint said. "Were you ever in the military?"

"The army, sir," Jerry said. "Two years."

"It shows."

"I can watch your back if you like, sir," Jerry said.

"Do you have a gun?"

"Well, no . . ."

"That's okay, Jerry," Clint said. "I appreciate the offer."

"Yes, sir. Good luck, sir."

"Well, with any luck," Clint said, "I'll just be having a talk with them."

But both men knew that probably wouldn't be true.

Irons and Brock watched Clint Adams leave the hotel and start down the street.

"Should we follow him?" Brock asked.

"No," Irons said. "We'll keep watch on the hotel to make sure the actress doesn't leave."

"What does Mr. Long see in her, anyway?" Brock asked. "She looks kind of scrawny."

"Have you ever seen her on stage?" Irons asked.

"No, but—"

"That explains why you don't see it," Irons said.

"But—"

"Also, the fact that you're an idiot."

"Hey—"

"Shut up, Brock," Irons said, "and keep your eyes on the front door."

TWENTY-SIX

Clint crossed the street on the corner, then started back to the doorway where the two men were secreted. He didn't take his gun out yet because he didn't want to attract undue attention. He'd have to take it out of his belt, though, when he got close, because he needed to get the drop on them if he was going to get them to talk.

When he got two doors away from them he slowed down. His back was to the wall. He reached behind him, pulled out his gun and began inching along.

Sarah watched from her window as Clint pressed himself against the wall and took out his gun. As he started to move along more slowly she tried to see the men he was after. Finally, she managed to pick them out of the shadows in a doorway almost directly across from her window. She couldn't see them clearly, but she did see some movement in the shadows, and she assumed this was where they were. If only she could see them, she could warn Clint if they were to produce guns.

Abruptly, she began looking to see if there was any way to open the hotel window. She reached over her head, looking for a latch, then to the sides, then to the top again.

From outside the window, it looked as if she were waving . . .

"What's that?" Brock asked.

"What's what?" Irons asked.

"That window, right over the front door," Brock said. "There's a woman waving her arms."

"What?" Irons looked up at the window and saw what Brock was talking about. There did seem to be a woman in a window, waving. In fact, it seemed to be . . .

"Hey," he said, "ain't that . . . the actress?"

"What?" Brock said. "I can't see. Wait . . ."

He stepped out of the doorway to get a better look. As he did he caught movement out of the corner of his eye. He turned, saw Clint almost on top of him and yelled, "Hey!"

And went for his gun.

Both men had guns in shoulder rigs. Clint watched one of them step out of the doorway, spot him and reach into his jacket. Since Clint's gun was already in his hand he knew the man didn't have a chance in hell.

"Don't!" he shouted, but he was too late.

He had no choice but to pull the trigger.

Irons watched as his partner went for his gun. There was a shot and Brock's chest seemed to explode. He was propelled back, his arms windmilling, blood spraying all over. As his partner's blood hit him in the face Irons went for his own gun, but he remained in the doorway.

And waited.

Sarah, having no idea that she was the cause, watched Clint shoot the man when he tried to draw his gun. Even from across the street she could see all the blood. Finally, she was able to see a second man in the doorway clearly as he drew his gun.

She wanted to call out to Clint to warn him, but knew he'd never be able to hear her with the window closed.

So instead, she screamed.

And fainted.

Clint watched the first man stagger back and fall, but he knew there was another one waiting for him in the doorway. He waited to see if the second man would step out, gun ready, but nothing happened. Suddenly, it seemed to get very quiet on the street. He looked across at the hotel, where people had stopped to stare, and they were like statues.

"What now?" he called out.

Nothing.

"Whoever you are, your partner's dead," Clint said, "and the police will be here soon. You might as well toss your gun out and step into the open."

There was still no answer, but Clint stayed alert.

Irons thought he'd be able to wait the man out, but when he heard the word *police,* he panicked. He cocked the hammer on his gun and stepped out, bringing the gun to bear.

When you've lived by the gun for as long as Clint Adams had, certain sounds become familiar. One was the sound of a hammer being cocked on a gun. Because of that sound, when Irons stepped out into the open and started bringing his gun around, Clint only had to pull the trigger of his own weapon to send a bullet into the man's chest. He reacted the same way his partner had: he stepped back, arms windmilling, a shocked look on his face, blood spurting from his chest—only he tripped over his fallen compadre and fell on top of him.

The two men were dead—and stacked like firewood.

TWENTY-SEVEN

When Jack Gallows and John Burton returned to the hotel, the bodies were still lying across the street, and Clint was being interviewed in the lobby by a police detective. Actually, the man's name was Lieutenant Andrew Donovan, and he'd been called in when the first policeman who responded to the scene discovered who Clint was.

"What is going on?" Burton asked, looking around the lobby at the gawking people.

"Let's find out," Gallows said.

He headed across the lobby to where Clint was sitting with the lieutenant, who looked up and instructed two uniformed policemen, "Keep those men back!"

"It's okay," Clint said, "they're with me."

"All right," Donovan said. "Let them through."

Donovan and Clint both stood up as Gallows and Burton reached them. The lieutenant was in his forties, a big man, easily topping six foot four, and very fit. He was wearing a three-piece suit and, in one hand, was holding Clint's gun.

"Lieutenant, this is the man I work for, Jack Gallows," Clint said. "And this is Miss Bernhardt's manager, John Burton."

"What happened here?" Burton demanded. "Is Sarah all right? Where is she?"

"Apparently," Donovan said, "Miss Bernhardt is fine. She didn't come out of her room during the shooting. I have a man staying upstairs with her now."

"Shooting?" Burton asked. "What shooting?"

"Those two men who followed us from the train station, they were here, across the street," Clint said. "When I tried to go over and talk to them, they threw down on me."

"Mr. Adams killed them both," Donovan said. "He says he had no choice. The doorman concurs. Says he watched the whole thing."

"Then what's the problem?" Gallows asked. "Are you holding Mr. Adams for any reason?"

"No, sir," Donovan said. "I'm just getting the whole story straight."

Burton asked, "May I go up and see Sarah?"

"I don't see why not," the lieutenant answered. "Officer, take Mr. Burton to Miss Bernhardt's room and tell the detective there that it's all right for him to see her."

"Yes, sir," the uniformed man said.

"We'll be up in a few minutes, John," Gallows said.

Burton nodded and hurried up the stairs, not bothering to wait for the elevator.

"Any reason why you're holding Mr. Adam's gun, Lieutenant?" Gallows asked.

Donovan looked at the gun in his hand, as if he'd forgotten about it.

"I guess not," he said, handing it back. "I was just wondering if he'd been walking the streets with it."

Clint accepted the gun back and said to Gallows, "I explained to the lieutenant that when I saw the men across the street I went back to my room to get my gun. I told him that I haven't been carrying a gun on his streets."

"What about you, Mr. Gallows?" Donovan asked.

"What about me, Lieutenant?"

"Are you carrying a gun?"

The lieutenant looked pointedly at the area beneath Gallows's right arm, where it was obvious to anyone who cared to look that he was carrying a gun in a shoulder rig.

"As you can plainly see, Lieutenant," Gallows said, pulling his jacket back to reveal the weapon, "I am."

"I'm sure you have the proper papers for that?"

"I do. I carry it as part of my job."

"And Mr. Adams doesn't have those same papers?"

"No, he doesn't," Gallows said. "We came here from Cleveland, and I hired him there. We haven't had the time to take care of it."

"Well," Donovan said, "it's nice to know that two men were killed on my streets by a law-abiding citizen like the Gunsmith."

"Lieutenant," Gallows said, "were you able to identify the two men?"

"We found papers in their pockets with their names," the policeman said. "David Irons and Sam Brock. Do you know them?"

"Never heard of them."

"Neither have I. Apparently, they're from Philadelphia."

"Philadelphia?" Gallows asked. "Not Cleveland?"

"No," Donovan said, "definitely Philadelphia."

Clint knew why this information was upsetting to Gallows. It meant that the men had followed Sarah all the way from Philadelphia, not just from Cleveland—and Jack Gallows had missed them.

"Any idea what they wanted?" Donovan asked.

"No," Gallows said, still perturbed.

"I never got a chance to ask them."

"And how much longer will you folks be in Chicago?"

"Miss Bernhardt has two performances," Gallows said. "Tonight and tomorrow night."

"And then you leave?"

"And then we leave."

"Very well," Donovan said. "Please try not to kill any-one else while you're here. Good day."

As he walked away, taking the uniformed men with him, Clint and Gallows faced each other.

"Got anything to tell me that you didn't tell him?" Gallows asked.

"Lots," Clint said.

TWENTY-EIGHT

Clint and Gallows went up to Sarah's room and found Burton there with her, along with the detective Donovan had sent up. Apparently, the lieutenant had forgotten to take his man with him.

"Everyone else is gone," Gallows said to the detective.

"Uh, am I supposed to go, too?"

"Well, we're here now, and it's our job to protect her," Gallows said, "so my guess would be . . . yes."

"Ma'am?" the detective said, looking at Sarah. She was seated on the divan with Burton, who was holding both her hands in his.

"Yes, detective," she said. "I'll be fine. Thank you."

"I'll be goin', then," the man said.

Gallows walked him to the door, said, "Thanks for your help," and closed it in his face.

When he turned it was to see Sarah launch herself into Clint Adams's arms.

"I thought I'd gotten you killed," she cried.

Clint hugged her for a moment, then held her at arm's length and looked at her.

"Whatever gave you that idea?"

"I . . . it was my fault they saw you," she said.

111

"You'd better sit down and explain that to me," Clint said.

They all sat and she explained how she thought she had attracted the gunmen's attention by flailing about in the window, causing them to step out of their hiding place and see Clint.

"I saw you shoot the first man and I wanted so much to warn you about the second, but I couldn't," she said. "I— I'm afraid, after that, I fainted."

"Sarah," Clint said, "it wasn't your fault. Not any of it."

"Do we know who those two men were?" Burton asked.

"We know their names," Gallows said, "and that they were from Philadelphia, but that's all."

"Philadelphia?" Burton asked. "They followed us from Philadelphia?"

"Apparently," Gallows said.

"And you did not see them?"

"No," Gallows said, with a scowl.

"Isn't that your job?"

"Yes, it is," Jack Gallows said, "and if I was you I'd fire my ass right now."

"Nonsense," Sarah said. She looked at Burton. "Don't even think about it, John."

Burton subsided.

"What do we do now?" she asked, looking at Clint and Gallows.

"Well," Gallows said, "we don't know what they wanted. We don't know if they worked for someone else. We don't even know if they would have done anything."

"The fact that they had guns and were quite willing to kill Mr. Adams, would suggest that they would have."

"Yes," Gallows said, "but I still think we should just continue on as planned."

"Well, of course we will," Burton said. "Sarah Bernhardt has never missed a performance."

"Sarah?" Clint asked. "Do you want to go on tonight? We can cancel the performance, you know."

"No, no," she said. "I wouldn't want to disappoint the people. I will go on as planned. In fact . . ." She stood up and smoothed down her skirt. "I should start getting ready. Gentlemen, if you please?"

The men all stood, but Burton seemed reluctant to leave.

"I think one of us should stay here with her, don't you?" he asked.

"I think you should all leave and let me get ready," she said. "I'll be fine."

"One of us will be outside the door, Miss Bernhardt," Gallows said to her. "Either Clint or me."

"There," she said to Burton, "I'll be perfectly safe."

"Well, all right . . ."

She saw the three men to the door, touched Clint on the arm as he went by and closed the door behind them.

"How could this have happened?" Burton demanded, turning on both the other men.

"How could what have happened, John?" Clint asked. "Nobody got near Sarah. For all we know those two men recognized me and were out to make a name for themselves."

Burton looked stunned.

"You mean . . . this may have had nothing at all to do with Sarah?" he asked.

"That's possible," Gallows said.

"Well . . ."

"The only one in any danger was Clint."

"And . . . and he is used to that," Burton said, "aren't you?"

"Yes, I am, John," Clint said. "Why don't you go to your room and get ready for the theater?"

"Yes," Burton said, "yes, I will. We can have dinner in the hotel before we go."

Suddenly, he seemed to feel much better about the situation. Clint and Gallows watched him walk down the hall and enter his room.

"You think those two were really after you?" Gallows asked.

"Not a chance," Clint said. "Who gets the door first, me or you?"

TWENTY-NINE

The two performances in Chicago went off without a hitch and Sarah Bernhardt—as was always the case—was brilliant. As far as Clint and Gallows could tell, there was no one else trailing them, and they all got on the train to St. Louis in a relatively relaxed state.

Frank Long didn't learn the fate of his men until he saw the newspaper the next afternoon. That was when he found out not only that they'd been shot to death on the street, but also that they were killed by Clint Adams. The newspaper went on to say that Adams was traveling with Sarah Bernhardt, acting as her bodyguard.

"Goddamnit!"

If he'd known that Clint Adams was Sarah's bodyguard he would never have employed two idiots like Irons and Brock.

"Sir?" the waiter asked. "Is the lunch all right?"

"It's fine," Long said. "Go away."

"Yes, sir."

Long knew Sarah Bernhardt's schedule by heart. He knew that her next performances were three nights at the Fox Theater in St. Louis. That meant he had plenty of time to hire more men, better men, before continuing on to St. Louis.

And he knew who to start with.

At the same time Clint, Gallows, Burton and Sarah Bernhardt were boarding the train to St. Louis, Long was meeting with Jarrod McKeever over breakfast.

"It's been a while since I've heard from you, Mr. Long," McKeever said.

"That's because I haven't been in need of your talents, Jarrod," Long said. "But now I am."

"What's the job?" McKeever asked, cutting into his inch-thick steak.

"Did you see the story in the *Tribune* about the shooting on the street?"

"The Gunsmith killin' two men? Yeah, I saw it." He stopped chewing and looked at Long. "Wait a minute. Were those your men?"

"They were," Long said, "but I had no idea who I was sending them up against."

"He killed them with two shots," McKeever said. "Stacked them on the street, it said in the paper. I wish I could have seen that."

"Jarrod," Long asked, "do you have any problem going up against the Gunsmith?"

"Me? Mr. Long, I got no trouble going up against anybody."

"That's good."

"Not for the right price."

"Oh," Long said, "the price will be right. In fact, it will be very generous."

"I just got one question."

"What is it?"

"Who else is with him?"

"Actually, he's working for another man, a detective named Jack Gallows."

"Gallows?"

"You know him?"

"Sure, I know him," McKeever said. "He's got offices right here in town."

"Is that a problem?"

"I'll need to hire another couple of men," McKeever said, "just to be on the safe side."

"That's no problem," Long said. "I'll cover all your expenses. Do we have a deal?"

"Almost."

Long sighed impatiently.

"What's the problem?"

"What's the job?" McKeever asked. "Exactly?"

"At some point," Long said, "I'm going to need to get past Adams and Gallows to get to Sarah Bernhardt."

"And you don't care how you do it?"

"Exactly."

McKeever cut off a huge hunk of steak, stuck it in his mouth and chewed it thoughtfully. He washed it down with a big swallow of coffee, then took his time refilling the cup. Long knew the man was making him wait, but he didn't care. McKeever's talents were worth the money he paid him and worth the extra time it sometimes took.

Also, the man was a killer, and Long did not treat him the way he treated anyone else. So he sat back, took a bite of his own food and waited.

"So, let me see if I have this right," Jarrod McKeever said, slowly. "I get to kill the Gunsmith, make a reputation for myself . . . and get paid for it?"

"That's exactly right."

"And what is it exactly that you have in mind for this actress?" McKeever asked.

"Well," Long said, "that part is none of your business. Do we have a deal?"

"Oh," McKeever said, "we have a deal."

THIRTY

On the train Clint and Gallows sat together, this time across the aisle from Sarah and Burton.

"Wait a minute," Clint said.

"What?"

"Isn't your office in Chicago?"

"Yeah."

"But . . . you never went there, did you?"

"I didn't have to."

"But . . . you were in town," Clint reasoned.

"The reason I go to my office is to get work," Gallows explained. "The reason I was in Chicago for the last two days was because I already had work. You see?"

"I see."

Clint was sitting near the window and Gallows was on the aisle. The big detective turned in his seat to look up and down the aisle.

"Anything?" Clint asked.

"No."

"Me, neither," Clint said. "I'm not even feeling anything."

"Neither am I," Gallows said. "It's odd."

"Yeah," Clint said. "Two men with guns and no back-up."

"And no replacements."

"Unless . . ."

"Unless what?" Gallows asked.

"Unless the replacements are waiting for us in St. Louis."

"That's possible, I guess," Gallows said. "What I'm wondering is if there are replacements, who's paying them?"

"Yeah, I've been thinking about that, too," Clint said. "I don't believe those two were just big fans of Sarah's."

"There'd be no reason for them to throw down on you," Gallows said. "No, there's somebody else behind this."

"Whatever *this* is."

"Right."

They rode in silence for a few moments, then Gallows said, "I'm still mad at myself, though."

"For what?"

"For letting those two follow us all the way from Philadelphia," the detective said. "That was careless on my part."

"You weren't expecting it," Clint said. "After all, you did think the job was protecting her from overexcited fans."

"Yeah, but still . . ." He looked across the aisle at Sarah and Burton. "To tell you the truth, this is the only job I've had in months. I'm lucky they didn't fire my ass."

"I still think we should fire him," Burton said.

"But why, John?"

"Allowing those ruffians to follow us from the East was not exactly what we hired him for."

"And what would you want to do to replace him at this stage?" she asked. "We wouldn't know who to ask."

"We could hire Mr. Adams," Burton said. "You seem to like him very much."

"I do," she said, "but he would be loyal to Mr. Gallows."

"We could pay him more than that man could."

"It wouldn't matter," she said. "Clint is friends with Mr. Gallows."

"Too friendly to take a well paying job?"

"Yes."

"You think these Americans hold loyalty in that high regard?" Burton asked.

"I think Clint would, yes."

"You think you know him that well?"

"Yes."

"Then you just want to keep Mr. Gallows on?" Burton asked.

"Yes, John, I do," she said. "I want to keep them both on. I have confidence in both of them."

Burton sighed.

"Very well," he said.

Sarah turned her head to look out the window, wishing that Clint would change seats with her manager.

After his meal with Frank Long, Jarrod McKeever went to the nearest Western Union office. He walked from the restaurant, so that when he arrived he knew who he wanted to send a telegram to and what he wanted to say.

McKeever was excited about the prospect of facing Clint Adams, man-to-man, in a gunfight. He knew he wasn't known at all west of the Mississippi, because most of the men he killed lived and died in places like Chicago, St. Louis, Cleveland, Wisconsin and Minnesota. It was time he built up a reputation in the West—before the old West was gone. What better way to do that than to kill one of the legends of the old West?

He needed someone to take care of Gallows, though, so that he could concentrate fully on Clint Adams. When he reached the telegraph office he wrote out a short message in pencil and handed it to the clerk. It would mean nothing to him, but it would mean something to the man who received it on the other end.

After that, he went to the train station and bought a ticket for the next train to St. Louis.

THIRTY-ONE

St. Louis, as a city, was somewhere between Chicago and Cleveland, but the Fox Theater dwarfed anything Sarah had yet seen in the United States.

This time all four of them went to the theater together. As soon as they walked in they were impressed by the sheer size of the place, and they hadn't even seen the auditorium yet.

"My God," she said.

"I heard about it," Burton said, "that is why I booked us in here for three nights, but . . . let's go and see the seating capacity."

They made their way through the lobby and when they entered the auditorium they were shocked into silence once again. Between the main floor, the mezzanine and the upper deck, the seating capacity was amazing.

And then there was the huge stage.

"My God," Sarah said.

Clint looked around. He really had nothing to compare it to. He'd been to small western theaters—like the Birdcage, in Tombstone—and he'd seen some theaters in San Francisco and Denver, but he really didn't know whether the size of this theater was unusual, as theaters went.

"Oh, yes," Sarah said, when he mentioned that. "This is an amazing theater." She turned to Burton. "Thank you for booking me here for three days, John."

"I was just working from word-of-mouth," he said. "Some people told me this was a special theater."

"This is as good as anything in New York," she said, "and better than most."

"I suppose we'd better find the manager," Burton said. "We need to work out some details."

"And we need to go over some security measures," Gallows said.

Sarah turned to him and asked, "Do you expect trouble here, Mr. Gallows?"

"Ma'am," he said, "I just want to be ready for it if it comes."

"That makes sense," she said, then added, "I suppose."

Once they had all spoken with the manager and had their own needs met, the next need was one they all shared—satisfying their hunger. The manager told them there was a place nearby called Number One Steakhouse, and Sarah immediately announced that was where they were going. When they got there—walking distance from the theater—the smell of cooking meat filled the air.

Sarah took one bite and announced that this was the best steak she'd ever had.

"What do you think, Clint?"

He was not as impressed.

"Sarah, wait until we get to cattle country," he said. "I think you'll be saying that a few more times."

"The chicken is very good, also," Burton said.

He had sworn off steak—and whiskey—since that night in Chicago when he'd sampled both. On the train he complained he could still smell the meat coming out of his pores. When Gallows pointed out that *beef* stroganoff was still meat, the smaller man had replied, "it's really not quite the same thing, is it?"

Sarah told Clint that if there was better steak than this farther west, she couldn't wait to get there.

While Clint, Gallows, Sarah and Burton were still eating, a train from Chicago pulled into Union Station. Jarrod McKeever stepped off and was met by a man of medium height, whose intense eyes often gave pause to much bigger men than he.

His name was Henry Brown. He claimed to be the Henry Brown who had worked for John Chisum and had ridden with Billy the Kid during the Lincoln County War. McKeever knew *that* Henry Brown was supposed to be dead almost four years now, lynched in Caldwell, Kansas, when he robbed a bank while wearing a lawman's badge. However, he didn't care one way or the other. All he knew was that this Henry Brown was fast with a gun and willing to work. They'd met several years before and had worked together successfully many times since then.

"Henry," McKeever said.

"Jarrod."

The two men shook hands.

"Who've you got with you?" McKeever asked.

Brown looked over his shoulder at two men who were lounging nearby.

"Them two," he said. "Lew Macklin and Terry Kern."

"Terry?" McKeever asked. "That's a girl's name."

"Don't tell him that," Henry Brown said, "but you can call him T.K. He likes that."

"Okay," McKeever said, "introduce me."

Brown made the introductions and McKeever shook hands with T.K. and Lew.

"We all know why we're here?" McKeever asked.

"To kill somebody, I hope," T.K. said.

"And get paid for it," Lew Macklin added.

"Well," Jarrod McKeever said, "before we can do that we've got to find them."

"You got any ideas where they might be?" Brown asked.

"As a matter of fact," McKeever said, "I do . . ."

Farther down the platform Frank Long detrained, carrying his own bag, but he was quickly met by a man who grabbed it from him.

"Got a buggy right out front, Mr. Long."

"In a minute."

Long watched McKeever talk first with one man, then with two more. They all wore guns. St. Louis was an odd town. At once a northern and southern town, it was also a cross between an eastern and western one. It was also as far west as Frank Long's work usually took him. But he was prepared to follow Sarah Bernhardt all the way to San Francisco if he had to.

"Sir?" the man asked.

Long looked at him and the man backed off and stood quietly, holding Long's bag.

"Put the bag in the buggy," Long said. "I'll be along."

"Yes, sir."

The young man hurried through the station and outside to the buggy. He'd never driven Frank Long before, but he'd heard stories about the man and, seeing him, was sure that every one was true.

Long waited until McKeever and his three men left the platform before he also did, walking outside to the waiting buggy.

THIRTY-TWO

Rather than overlooking Chestnut Street, which was in front of the Hotel Regal, Sarah's room had a breathtaking view of the Mississippi River. Clint stood at the window and stared at the muddy river. Behind him he could hear Sarah and Burton discussing her performance for the next three nights.

"Doesn't matter how many times I see it," Gallows said, coming up next to Clint.

"I know," Clint said. "It's an amazing thing, the way it . . . moves, changes course, all on its own."

"What are you two talking about?" Sarah asked, coming up behind them. They moved to allow her to stand between them and look out the window.

"The Mississippi," Clint said.

"Oh, my," Sarah breathed. "I'm already finding St. Louis a very interesting city. First the theater and now this."

"That's the longest river in the world," Gallows said.

"No," Clint said, "I think that's the Amazon."

"Amazon?" Gallows asked. "Where the hell is that?"

"South America," Clint said.

"It's longer than the Mississippi?"

"I think so," Clint said. "Even if I'm wrong, they're the two longest rivers in the world."

"But the Mississippi is the longest in this country," Gallows said.

"Without a doubt."

"What is that area down there called?" Sarah asked. She was pointing to a collection of buildings across from the hotel.

"They call that the Landing," Clint said. "There are bars and restaurants there. It's frequented by a lot of people from the docks."

"Not a place for a lady," Gallows told her.

"Is there anyplace where a lady could walk along the water?" Sarah asked.

"Sure there us," Gallows said, giving Clint a look, "but I don't think that's such a good idea, right now."

She looked at Gallows, then Clint, then the detective again.

"You're still worried because of those men with the guns in Chicago?"

"I'm just tryin' to do my job, Miss Bernhardt," Gallows said. "I think you should stay in your suite as much as possible until your first performance."

"But that's not until tomorrow night," she said.

"I agree with Mr. Gallows, Sarah," Burton said from across the room. "It's better to be on the safe side."

She turned to look at Burton, then stared back out the window.

"I can't argue with all three of you," she said, forlornly.

At that moment Frank Long was in the bar of his hotel, which was several blocks from the Regal. It was called The St. Louis Inn. He was nursing a glass of brandy and still had half of it when Jarrod McKeever walked in. He went to the bar, got himself a beer and then joined Long at his table.

"I saw you with your three men," Long said.

"Don't worry," McKeever said. "Two of them come cheap."

"I'm not worried about the money," Long said, "as long as they can do the job."

"They'll do it," McKeever said.

"Where are they now?"

"They're in a bar on the Landing," McKeever said. "A dive called the Bucket of Blood." The man laughed. "There's always a dive called the Bucket of Blood. They're waitin' for me to tell them exactly what the job is."

"Well," Frank Long said, "in that case listen up, because I'm about to fill you in."

THIRTY-THREE

Jarrod McKeever went alone to check out the Fox Theater, which he knew next to nothing about. He was not a theater-goer. He preferred saloons. It did not take him long to figure out the Fox was a bad place to try and do what Frank Long wanted to do. But before reporting back to Long, McKeever decided to wait one night. He wanted to see Sarah Bernhardt's first performance and scope out her transportation to and from the theater, before he made his final report. And until that time, he decided to leave Henry Brown and his two partners in the Bucket of Blood, where they couldn't do any harm.

McKeever was a big man, but when he wanted to follow someone and go unnoticed, he knew how to do it.

Clint and Gallows decided, after the incident in Chicago, that the four of them should travel to and from the theater together. Burton wouldn't be much good in a fight, but he was added insulation for Sarah. The four stayed close together when they walked from the hotel to the cab keeping her in their midst and did the same going from the cab to the stage door of the theater. During the performance Clint

131

and Gallows remained in the wings—stage left and stage right—while Burton sat out front.

The St. Louis audience had turned out in droves to see the Divine Sarah, and the place was packed to the rafters. Afterward, the applause was deafening.

The evening was a great success.

McKeever chafed beneath his starched collar as he stood in the back of the theater and watched. He moved around once the lights had dimmed and the performance had begun. He spotted both Clint and Gallows at their positions. And he even had time to notice that Sarah Bernhardt was beautiful and very good at what she did.

What he didn't see was a way to get to her, and that was what he was going to report to Frank Long.

At dinner in the hotel, Sarah was still flushed from her triumph.

"You were fabulous," Burton told her for the tenth time.

"And why not?" she asked. "A fabulous theater and a fabulous crowd should get a fabulous performance."

Burton had ordered champagne, and when they killed the first bottle he ordered a second.

"The Fox already wants us to add two more performances," Burton said, "and they've offered us a lot of money."

"Two more days in St. Louis?" Gallows asked.

"One more day," Burton said. "They want a matinee."

"One more day, two more performances," Clint said. "Won't that be exhausting?"

Burton leaned forward. "Didn't you hear me when I said they offered us a lot of money?"

"We have obligations in Kansas City, John," Sarah reminded him.

"In a small, Kansas City theater," Burton reminded her. "Nothing like the Fox Theater."

"Nevertheless," Sarah said, "as pleased as I am with the Fox, I intend to honor my obligations. We will be leaving for Kansas City as scheduled."

Both Clint and Gallows expected more of a fight from her manager, but he simply shrugged and said, "All right, I will tell them we can't do it. But they might not understand an artist who actually cares about her obligations more than she does about money."

"They will get over it," Sarah said. "And now, if you gentlemen will excuse me, I think I'm going to go to my room and rest."

"I'll walk you up," Clint said.

"Don't forget," Gallows said, "we're meeting in the bar to talk about tomorrow."

"I'll be there," Clint said, pulling Sarah's chair out for her.

Jarrod McKeever watched as Clint Adams walked Sarah Bernhardt across the lobby. He could have challenged Adams right there, but that would not go over big with the law in St. Louis. He also could have tried to grab the actress, but that would have been easier if she'd been with one of the other men, not Adams.

McKeever sighed. Frank Long was not going to like what he had to tell him.

He turned and left the hotel.

Clint stopped with Sarah at her door and she asked, "Would you like to come in?"

They had still not resolved that whole business of "having a moment" in Chicago.

"Jack's waiting for me in the bar," Clint told her. "And I know that you understand about keeping one's obligations."

"I certainly do," she said, "but a girl doesn't necessarily like to have her own words used against her, Clint."

She stood on her toes to kiss his cheek.

"I'll remember that," he promised.

THIRTY-FOUR

Frank Long was with another Sarah Bernhardt look-alike whore when Jarrod McKeever knocked on his hotel room door.

"Shat the hell—" she said.

Long slapped her on the ass and said, "Don't move."

"Hey!" she complained, looking over her shoulder at him. "If you left a mark that's gonna cost you extra." She rubbed her right buttock.

"I'll pay you double," he said, getting off the bed.

"Ooh," she asked, "wanna smack the left one?"

"We'll talk about it."

Unlike Chicago, Long had a suite at this hotel, so when he opened the door McKeever was unable to see the whore—which didn't mean he didn't know she was there. As a matter of fact, it was he who helped Long get her.

"Am I interrupting?" he asked.

"Yeah, but come in anyway."

McKeever entered and Long closed the door. He didn't seem to mind that he was naked, and that his penis was still erect, so McKeever didn't mention it.

"What have you got?" Long asked.

"Not much," McKeever said.

"What do you mean?"

"I don't think you should make a move on her in St. Louis," McKeever said. "There's too much that can go wrong."

"Kansas City, then?"

"I've given this a lot of thought," McKeever said. "Didn't you say they'd be playing the Birdcage in Tombstone?"

"That's right."

"That's the place to do it."

"Tombstone?"

"Right," McKeever said. "After what that town's been through, it won't be such a big thing as it might be in one of these cities."

"I've . . . never been to Tombstone," Long said.

"Frank, you've never been west of the Mississippi River, have you?" McKeever asked.

"No."

McKeever slapped Long on the back and said, "It'll be a new experience for you."

Long looked dubious.

"Don't worry," McKeever said. "Your money's just as good there as here."

He slapped Long on the back again.

"Don't you have a whore in the other room?" he asked.

"Uh, yeah," Long said, "yeah . . ."

"You better get back to it, then," McKeever said. "We'll talk tomorrow."

Clint found Gallows waiting for him in the bar, armed with two beers.

"Got you one so you wouldn't have to wait," he said, pushing one toward Clint.

"Where's Burton?"

"Went to his room," Gallows said.

"Thought you'd pass him on the way."

"I didn't."

"Maybe he made a stop," Gallows said. "Listen, I wanted to talk about tonight and tomorrow. Even though we're not in Chicago, I think we should stay outside her room again. I mean, I was doing it in Cleveland, for Chrissake, might as well keep doing it."

"I agree," Clint said.

"Good," Gallows said. "I'll take the first watch and you can relieve me around three A.M."

"That's good."

"Now, about tomorrow . . ." Gallows said, and they went on to discuss security for the next day.

McKeever looked into the bar and saw Clint and Gallows standing there holding beers. He was tempted to go inside, have a beer and keep an eye on them, but that would be playing with fire. Better for them not to see him until he was ready.

He decided instead to go over to the Bucket of Blood and have a beer with Henry Brown and his boys.

Long hesitated before going back in to the whore. In fact, he walked to the window and looked out at the river. It was true he'd never been west of the Mississippi. He'd made his fortune in the East and had been plying it there for years. This was the farthest west he had ever come, but when he considered the prize he was after it seemed worth it. Besides, he'd have McKeever and his men with him. He knew McKeever had been west, and the other men certainly looked like westerners.

Sure, then, why not? If that's where Sarah Bernhardt was going, and that's where McKeever thought they had the best chance, then he'd go.

Maybe it was time for Frank Long to make his mark in the West, anyway.

THIRTY-FIVE

Clint relieved Jack Gallows at three A.M. and at three-thirty the door to Sarah's room opened.

"I thought I'd find you here," she said.

He stood up from the chair he was sitting in and asked, "Is everything all right?"

"No."

"What's wrong?"

She reached out, grabbed ahold of the front of his shirt and pulled him into the room. She closed the door, then turned to face him.

"We have unfinished business."

He noticed she was in her nightgown.

"Sarah . . ."

"Shut up."

She threw her arms around his neck, pulled him down to her and kissed him on the mouth. Surprised, he didn't react immediately, but when he finally did, it was to gather her into his arms and lift her off the floor. She moaned as the kiss deepened, and he turned to carry her into the bedroom of the suite.

After all, what better way to keep an eye on her?

• • •

"I don't get it," T.K. said to McKeever.

"What don't you get?"

"What's he want with her?"

"Have you ever seen her?" McKeever asked. "Onstage?"

"No," T.K. said.

Lew Macklin laughed.

"We ain't been to too many theaters, have we, T.K.?" he asked.

"Not if it ain't in the saloon," T.K. said.

"Well, then, you guys'll be glad to hear we're goin' to Tombstone," McKeever said.

"Tombstone?" Henry Brown asked. "What for?"

"Because she's gonna be playin' the Birdcage," McKeever said, "and it's gonna be a lot easier to get to her there than here."

"Tombstone," Lew Macklin said, excitedly. "Think we'll see Doc Holliday there?"

"Holliday's dead, you idiot," Brown said.

"What about Wyatt Earp?" T.K. asked.

"Earp ain't gonna be there, either," Brown said. "What's wrong with you guys? Ain't you ever been west of the Mississippi before?"

"Well," Macklin said, "no."

McKeever looked at Brown.

"Don't worry," Brown said, "we can dig up some more men when we get there. When're we leavin'?"

"Well," McKeever said, "they ain't gonna be in Tombstone for a while. They still got to go to Kansas City, Oklahoma City and Fort Worth. Maybe another Texas stop."

"How long's that gonna take?" Brown asked.

"Probably a couple of weeks."

"And what are we gonna do in the meantime?"

McKeever rubbed his jaw.

"I don't know," he said, finally. "Follow along behind them?"

"Seems to me it'd be smarter to just go to Tombstone

and wait for them," Brown said. "That way we'd get the lay of the land and hire a few more men before they even got there."

McKeever stared at Brown.

"I don't know why I never gave you credit for brains before, Henry," he said.

"You ain't never asked me for an idea before."

"Well," McKeever said, "this is a good one. There's just one thing you and I have to do before we leave."

"What's that?" Brown asked.

McKeever took out some of the money Frank Long had given him, tossed it across the table at T.K. and Macklin, and said, "Hey, boys—you're fired!"

When Clint peeled off Sarah's nightdown he was delighted to find that her small breasts were pink-tipped, firmer than he'd first thought, like a couple of small, ripe peaches. Also, her skin was pale, as was the hair between her legs.

"Guess what?" she said, pulling his shirt off.

"What?" he asked.

"I think we're having another moment."

He laughed, palmed her breasts, rubbing the nipples and lifting them to his mouth.

"Sarah," he said, "we're going to have a lot of moments tonight."

McKeever had to stand up and face the two men before they accepted the fact that they were fired. Reluctantly, they picked up the little bit of money he'd tossed them and left the bar.

"Now what?" Brown asked.

"Now we go and tell the boss our idea," McKeever said, "and get the money for our train fare."

"Train? Why don't we just ride? We got the time."

"The sooner we get to Tombstone, the faster we get set up."

"Good point," Brown said. "Mind if I tag along?"

"Why not?" McKeever said. "You got to meet him, sometime."

The whore was sucking Frank Long's wet cock, moaning and cupping his balls in her hand. She didn't even care when he grabbed her hair and called her Sarah. For the amount of money he was paying her, he could have called her Mary Lincoln and she wouldn't have cared.

She could feel him swelling in her mouth, so she slid her hands beneath his buttocks and, with surprising strength for a gal so slender, actually lifted his butt off the bed. She took the entire length of his penis into her mouth, did something with her tongue and suddenly he was exploding. She expertly accommodated his entire emission and before he was even done there was a loud knocking at the door.

She released him from her mouth and rolled onto her back.

"Somebody at the door," she said, wiping an errant drop from the corner of her mouth with her fingers.

"Goddamnit," he said, gutturally.

This time when he got up he donned a robe before going to the door. When he opened it and saw McKeever there with another man he said, "What the hell—"

"Frank," McKeever said, "this is Henry Brown, and we need some money tonight."

"For what?"

McKeever smiled and said, "We're going to Tombstone."

THIRTY-SIX

Clint kissed Sarah Bernhardt's nipples, licked them, swirled his tongue around them until she moaned and then bit them. He then kissed his way down her taut belly until his face was nestled between her legs. She gasped at the first touch of his tongue and reached down to hold his head.

"Oh, God, yes," she said, as he licked her avidly. She couldn't keep still. Writhing beneath him, she released his head but gathered up two fistfuls of sheet and held on tightly. When the waves of pleasure finally washed over her, inundating her, she could stay quiet no longer and she cried out . . .

Long allowed McKeever to explain the idea of going to Tombstone ahead of the Bernhardt party and during that time got his breathing back under control. Still, he had to clear his throat before speaking again.

"Whataya think?" McKeever asked.

"I think this could've waited until morning," Long said. "Meet me in the dining room downstairs for breakfast at nine and we'll discuss it further."

"What's to discuss?" McKeever asked.

143

"Whether or not I'll go ahead with you," Long said and slammed the door in their faces.

When he turned, the whore was standing in the doorway of the bedroom, half dressed.

"Can I have my money now?"

"What do you mean?" Long asked. "We are not finished."

"Really?" she asked, looking surprised.

"Get your ass back in that bed," he said, dropping his robe to the floor.

She was surprised to see that he was either still fully erect or hard again.

"You know," she said, admiringly, "for a fella your size you got a lot of stamina."

He was going to fuck her brainless for that remark.

"I'm so embarrassed," Sarah said, when she got her breath back.

"About what?" Clint asked.

"My legs."

"What's wrong with them?" he asked, running his hands over her smooth thighs.

"I lost control of them," she said. "You had me kicking . . . I couldn't stop! Where did you learn to do that to a girl?"

"You seemed to like what I was doing," he said, "so I kept on doing it."

"Well," she said, sliding her hand down over his belly, "you know, two can play at that game."

When she took his penis in her hand, it was already hard. She slid down on the bed until she was between his legs and then she began to stroke him with one hand while fondling his testicles with the other. Playfully, she flicked her tongue out to lick him quickly, on the underside, just beneath the head of his penis. He jumped as her tongue touched him, and she laughed.

"Ah," she said, "you're sensitive there. I find that so very . . . arousing."

"Sarah—"

"Shh," she said, and licked the entire length of him, from his balls back to the head, and then concentrated on that tender spot again.

Next she used her hands: first to tenderly hold his balls and kiss them; then to wrap both of them around his full length so she could lick the head, wetting it thoroughly.

Finally, she slid her lips over his shaft and took him into her mouth. He lifted his hips and said, "I think I'm really going to enjoy these moments!"

THIRTY-SEVEN

Clint woke during the night and looked at Sarah lying beside him. She was on her belly and completely uncovered. He took a moment to admire her skin, and the way the line of her back flowed into her buttocks before pulling the bedsheet up to cover her.

Clasping his hands behind his head, Clint stared at the ceiling and wondered if this would have happened if he'd had the first watch of the night. If that had been the case he would have had to leap out of bed, get dressed and position himself outside Sarah's door before Jack Gallows left his room to come down the hall and relieve him. So, if this was going to happen again over the course of the rest of the trip—and without anyone knowing about it—it would only be on the nights when he had the second watch.

As it stood, he was going to have to make sure he woke early enough in the morning to get himself in front of her door before Gallows and Burton rose for the day. And since she had not dragged him into her room until three-thirty, that meant that he would have to get up . . . well, now!

Clint had just about gotten his butt onto the chair when the door to Jack Gallows's room opened and the detective stepped out. He looked down the hall, saw Clint and came walking over.

"How was your night?"

"Uneventful," Clint lied.

"Do you want to knock on her door and get her up?" Gallows asked. "Then we can go and have breakfast?"

"No," Clint said, "let her sleep and get up when she's ready. She's got all day to get ready for tonight's performance."

"Well, I'm hungry," Gallows said, "so I'll go down and have breakfast. If she's not up by the time I'm done, I'll come back and spell you so you can eat."

"That's fine," Clint said. "Enjoy."

He watched Gallows walk down the hall. The moment the detective disappeared on the steps leading down to the lobby Clint let his head settle back against the door behind him and closed his eyes. His sleep was short-lived, though, as about twenty minutes later the door to Burton's room opened, waking him.

"Not awake yet?" Burton asked.

For a moment Clint thought the man was commenting on his appearance, but then realized he was talking about Sarah.

"Not yet," Clint said. "I haven't heard any movement inside."

"Well," Burton said, "I am going to go and have some breakfast. We'll just let her sleep."

"Yes, sir."

He watched Burton walk down the hall and, as with Gallows, as soon as the man was out of sight, Clint put his head back and closed his eyes. This time it was half an hour before he was awakened, and this time it was the door behind him opening that did it.

"Oh, you poor man," Sarah said, leaning over and kissing him. "I kept you up most of the night."

"Not really," Clint said. "I got some sleep before I relieved Jack. How are you this morning?"

"I'm wonderful," she said. "Would you like to come in?"

"I'd like to," he said, "but I don't think I should. Jack and Burton have both already gotten up and gone down to breakfast and, to tell you the truth, I'm starving."

She giggled and said, "Actually, so am I. I'll get dressed quickly and maybe we can join them before they're done."

"Sounds like a good plan," Clint said.

"Would you like to come inside and wait while I dress?"

"I would," he said, "but I don't trust myself. If I come in, we'll never get to breakfast."

"You're a sweet man," she said. "I'll hurry."

A few blocks away, Frank Long entered his hotel's dining room and found both Jarrod McKeever and the other man—Henry Brown, although he didn't know his name at that moment—waiting for him. When he joined them, McKeever made the introductions.

"It was Henry's idea that we go ahead to Tombstone and just wait," McKeever added.

"Well, I've decided it's a good one," Long said.

He paused to order his breakfast when the waiter came over. The other two men had already ordered.

"So you're comin' with us?" McKeever asked.

"Yes," Long said, "but as you pointed out, I have never been that far west. What will I need?"

"Don't worry," McKeever said, "whatever you need you can get there. What I suggest we do is get over to Union Station today and get the first train out west."

"Very well," Long said. "After breakfast."

Ultimately, Long thought this would work. It was better than chasing Sarah Bernhardt around the country, waiting for the proper moment to act. Arriving in Tombstone ahead

of her and her party—and well ahead of them, at that—
would enable them to get everything in place.

For the first time Frank Long actually thought he had a
solid plan that would work.

THIRTY-EIGHT

Clint and Sarah found Gallows and Burton still at breakfast when they came down.

"There's the late riser," Burton said. He rose quickly to hold Sarah's chair for her.

"Good morning, John," she said. "Mr. Gallows."

"I think at this point," Gallows said, "you should probably start calling me Jack, ma'am."

"Only," she countered, "if you agree to stop calling me *ma'am* or *Miss Bernhardt*."

"I agree, ma—uh, Sara."

From the look of their plates—if they had both eaten at the same rate—Gallows had probably ordered first, and then Burton a bit later. Both, however, still had food on their plates. Clint beckoned to the waiter, who quickly came over and took his order of steak and eggs for both himself and Sarah.

"Did everyone sleep well?" Gallows asked.

"I must say," Sarah replied, "I haven't had a night like last night in quite a while."

Clint hoped there was nothing showing on his face, because he was nowhere near the actor Sarah was.

"That's good," Burton said. "You do look well rested."

151

"Thank you."

"On the other hand," Gallows said to Clint, "you look like crap."

"Thanks a lot."

The waiter came with their breakfast at that point, after which Clint managed to change the subject.

When they had all finished eating, Burton told Sarah he had some business he wanted to discuss with her.

"Could we go to your suite and do it?"

"Of course, John," she said. "We don't want to bore these gentlemen with our business. Will you both excuse us?"

"Of course," Gallows said. "We'll have some more coffee."

Sarah and Burton left, and when Clint and Gallows had another pot of coffee on the table, Gallows said, "I'm glad they left. I have somethin' I wanna talk to you about, too."

"The man in the theater last night?"

"How did you know?" Gallows asked. "I mean, there were a lot of men in the theater last night."

"The one who looked so uncomfortable in his suit," Clint said. "The one who kept walking around the theater, trying to get a look at you and me."

"The one who thought nobody was noticing him."

"Right," Clint said. "Did you recognize him?"

"Actually," Gallows said, "I might have."

"Who was it?"

"Well, I'm not sure," Gallows said, "but I think it might have been a fella named Jarrod McKeever."

"And who is McKeever?"

"A gun for hire."

"Uh-huh," Clint said. "An eastern gun or a western gun?"

"Just a gun," Gallows said. "McKeever is an equal opportunity shootist."

"So," Clint said, "you think McKeever was hired by whoever had hired those other two I killed?"

"Could be."

"I guess we better keep an eye out for this guy," Clint said, "and approach him much more carefully than I did those other two."

"I've got another idea," Gallows said. "I'm gonna send a telegram to Chicago and see if McKeever has been seen around."

"That's a good idea," Clint said. "I'll stay near the hotel, take a walk around outside and see what I can see."

"As long as we stay with her," Gallows said, "nobody should be able to get to her."

"Depending on what it is they want to do," Clint said.

"What do you mean?"

"I mean if somebody really wants to . . . hurt her, there's not much we can do to stop it."

"You don't mean hurt her," Gallows said, "you mean kill her."

"I mean like a rifle on a rooftop."

Gallows nodded.

"Can't do much to defend that," he agreed. "Only . . . why would somebody want to do that?"

"I don't know," Clint said. "Come on, we might as well get started."

They paid the bill—Gallows wrote Burton's room number on the check—then walked through the lobby and left the hotel. Outside they split up, agreeing to meet back in the lobby in an hour. Gallows went in search of a telegraph office, and Clint went for a walk around the hotel.

At that moment Frank Long, Henry Brown and Jarrod McKeever were boarding a train from Union Station. It would take them to Kansas City, where they'd switch for a train west.

Their absence from the scene for the rest of Sarah Bernhardt's stay in St. Louis would convince Clint and Gallows
that they were wrong about Jarrod McKeever. In fact, it
would give them a false sense of security for the rest of the
tour—until the party came to Tombstone, Arizona.

THIRTY-NINE

The next two performances at the Fox Theater went better than the first. By the time Sarah Bernhardt left St. Louis she was the toast of the city. The word reached Kansas City about how good she was, so that city turned out in impressive numbers to see her. The theater was not as impressive, but it was packed just the same. And the same went for Oklahoma City, and Fort Worth, and some other one-night stops in between.

During that time Clint and Sarah were able to be together almost every other tonight. They got into the habit of timing their lovemaking so that they also got enough sleep. There were no other mornings when Clint "looked like crap" at breakfast.

Gallows's telegram to Chicago revealed very little about Jarrod McKeever, which was okay. As far as Clint and Gallows were concerned, the incident in the theater was something they had misinterpreted. Just an uncomfortable man trying to walk it off.

By the time they arrived in Tombstone by stagecoach from the town of Fairbank—which was the nearest railhead, nine miles away—neither Clint nor Jack Gallows had felt the presence of anyone following them since St. Louis.

As they stepped down from the coach John Burton heaved a sigh of relief.

"You mean to tell me people used to travel hundreds of miles over this terrain in conveyances like this?"

"All the time," Gallows said.

Clint reached up to help Sarah step down from the coach. Gallows was catching the luggage as it was being dropped from the top. This was virtually the first stop on the tour where there were no porters to help with the bags. That meant that everyone was going to have to carry something.

"Here ya go, John."

When Burton turned, Gallows tossed him one of the smaller bags. Burton threw his hands up, not to catch it but to shield himself. The bag struck him and then hit the ground. He staggered back a few steps before regaining his balance.

"Hey!"

"Sorry," Gallows said. "I just thought you'd . . . catch it."

"I don't know how to . . . catch it," Burton said.

"Well," Gallows said, "you can pick it up."

Burton looked around. There had been a load of people on the large stage, and there were other people meeting them. There were also townspeople just standing around watching.

"Perhaps we can hire some help," Burton said.

"We can handle it if we all carry something," Gallows said.

"Even Sarah?" Burton asked. "You expect Sarah Bernhardt to carry her own—"

"I can take this small one, John," she said, picking up the bag at his feet. "You take something larger."

Muttering, Burton picked up a bag only slightly larger than the one she was carrying. Gallows had one in each hand and one under his arm. Clint held one in his left hand

and one under his left arm, leaving his gun hand free. After all, they weren't in the east anymore, and this was Tombstone. The shots from the O.K. Corral were still echoing here.

They walked down Allan Street to the nearest hotel, across from the Alhambra Saloon and down the street from the Oriental. The Birdcage, Clint knew, was still several blocks away.

The hotel was called the Four Kings and hadn't been there the last time Clint was in town. They had a reservation for Sarah Bernhardt and her company, and the young clerk was very excited that they were there.

"Everyone in town is waiting to see you, Miss Bernhardt," he gushed to her.

"That's very nice," she said, as Burton signed them all in. "Thank you."

"I can have someone take your bags up to your rooms," the clerk offered.

"That would be excellent," Burton said.

The clerk came around from behind the desk.

"I can show Miss Bernhardt to her room personally," he said, then added, "Oh, and the rest of you, as well."

"Thanks so much," Clint said.

"Please, follow me."

The hotel across the street was called the Palace. Upon arrival in town, Frank Long had taken four rooms, two of which overlooked Allan Street. Since that time someone was always at the window of one of those rooms, waiting for the stage to arrive. Today it was George Fagen. He and a man named Lane Borcher had been hired by Brown the day after he, Long and McKeever had gotten to town. He'd found them in the Oriental Saloon.

Sarah Bernhardt had been described to each man, so they'd know her when she got off the stage. It also helped that she had three men with her. Fagen watched, and when he saw them go into the Four Kings, he left the room to go and find Henry Brown. As far as he and Borcher knew, that's who they worked for.

FORTY

Henry Brown was in the Oriental Saloon with Jarrod Mc-
Keever when the stage pulled in.

"Where's Long?" Brown asked.

"In his room with a whore."

"One that looks like her?"

"As close as he can get."

"Don't he ever get tired?" Brown asked. "I mean, I like
pussy as much as the next guy, but . . ."

"I don't think he does get tired," McKeever said. "To
tell you the truth, I'm kinda jealous."

"Yeah," Brown admitted, "me, too."

At that moment, George Fagen walked in. He spotted
Brown and McKeever and approached them.

"They're here," he said. "The woman and three men.
Only two of the men were armed. Just got in and went to
the Four Kings."

"Okay," McKeever said. "This is it. I'll go and tell Long
they're here. You might as well wait here. And you," he
said, pointing to Fagen, "find your partner and get him over
here."

Fagen still didn't really know who McKeever was, so he
looked at Brown, who nodded.

"Do it," he said.

"Right."

As McKeever left the saloon to go over to the hotel, he thought it might be time to let Fagen and Borcher know who was really in charge.

The whore rolled over, breathing heavily.

"Wait, wait," she said, holding her hand out to Long. "I need a minute."

"Come on," Long said.

He was kneeling on the bed, a huge erection jutting out from between his legs.

"Mister," she said, "I don't know how you do it. I've taken on whole bunkhouses of cowboys that don't take as much out of me as you do."

Long didn't care what she had to say. They'd been in Tombstone for almost two weeks and the only thing that managed to fend off his impatience was sex. Usually, it was with this blond whore who came the closest to resembling Sarah Bernhardt, but there were times when he used some of the others. He had become the best customer at Miss Amy's whorehouse, and she never balked at sending a whore—sometimes two—to his hotel.

"Are all the men from back East like you?" she asked, parting her legs and bracing herself to receive him.

"No," he said. "Just me."

He knelt between her legs and drove himself into her . . .

George Fagen found Lane Borcher in the Alhambra Saloon, playing roulette.

He came up behind him and said, "Time to go."

"Wait a minute," Borcher said. "You got any money?"

"No."

"Come on," he said, "I been playing number eight all day. It's gonna come in."

"What makes you think it's gonna come in now?"

"I just need twenty dollars."

"How much you been betting?"

"Five each time," Borcher sad. "If I put twenty on it now and it comes in, I'll be ahead. Come on, you got twenty dollars."

"Not for that, I don't," Fagen said, "Come on, the boss is waitin'."

Borcher looked over at the wheel, which was turning, and at the white ball, which was going around.

"No more bets," he heard, as Fagen dragged him away.

As they went out the door the ball dropped onto the wheel, bounced around a few times, and came to a stop on number eight.

McKeever could hear the girl yelling when he got to the second floor of the hotel. He didn't have to guess which room she was in. When he got to the door she sounded like she was reaching a peak, so he hesitated before knocking. Then he heard a man roar—or maybe it was a bull. The two voices went on for a few moments, then faded out, and he took that as a signal to bang on the door.

When Long answered the door McKeever was glad he'd taken the time to pull on a pair of pants. Behind him, on the bed, a blond whore was sprawled across the bed on her back. She wasn't dead, because he could see that she was breathing hard. McKeever wondered if you could kill a whore with sex.

"What is it?"

"She's here," McKeever said. "Your girl is here."

"Where?"

"The Four Kings."

Long ran his hand over his face. At least the guy was breathing hard, himself.

"All right," Long said. "Get everyone together and bring them up here tonight. It's time we told them all what we have in mind."

FORTY-ONE

"Wait a minute," Henry Brown said.

All the other men at the table in the Oriental looked at him. They had all met at a back table, and when Frank Long walked in they stared at him as he approached them and sat down.

"Boys," Brown had said, "this is the boss, Frank Long."

It had taken them a while to get used to the idea, but after that they all listened to his story. In the end, it was Henry Brown who spoke up.

"You just . . . want her?"

"That's right."

"For you own?"

"Right again."

Brown looked at McKeever, who just shrugged.

"You want us to grab one of the most famous actresses in the world just because you . . . what? You're a fan?"

"That's right," he said, "I'm a fan and more."

Brown looked around the table.

"Jarrod?"

"Hey," McKeever said, "it's his money. He can spend it

163

any way he wants. If he wants to kidnap this actress so he can take her out every once in a while and make her perform, what do I care? I'm gettin' paid."

"You boys?" Brown asked Fagen and Borcher.

"Hey," Borcher said, "you brought us in and said there was a lot of money to be made."

"And there is," Long said. "I'll pay you all generously for this."

"That's all we care about," Fagen said.

"So I guess that leaves you, Mr. Brown," Long said.

Brown hesitated, then shrugged and said, "Well, if nobody else thinks it's weird . . ."

"Good," Long said. "Now there is only the question of Clint Adams."

"The Gunsmith?" Borcher asked. "He's involved with this?"

"He's one of the men guarding her," Long said.

Borcher and Fagen both looked at Brown, like there was something he hadn't told them.

"The Gunsmith is my concern," McKeever said. "The rest of you only have to deal with the other two men."

"And who are they?" Fagen asked.

"One of them is her manager, a guy named Burton," Long said. "He came with her from England."

"And the other one?" Borcher asked.

"You fellas ever hear of a man named Jack Gallows?"

"Gallows?" Fagen repeated. "Never heard of him."

"Me, neither," Borcher said. "Who is he?"

"A detective from Chicago," McKeever said.

"Not a gun for hire?" Brown asked.

"No."

"And that's it?" Brown asked. "That's all of it?"

"That's all of it," Long said.

"So when do you want us to do this?" Brown asked.

"Tomorrow night," Long said, "after her performance."

"And do you have this planned out?" Brown asked.

"No," Long said, "that will be up to Mr. McKeever. He will do the planning."

"And where will you be during all this?" Brown asked.

"I will be wherever Mr. McKeever tells me to be waiting," Long said. "We will be leaving immediately with Miss Bernhardt."

"To go where?" Brown asked.

"I will be taking her back East with me," Long said. "Mr. McKeever will accompany me. The rest of you will be paid off before we leave. After that, you may do whatever you please."

"How much?" Borcher asked.

Long told them.

"Is that . . . each?" Fagen asked.

"Yes," Long said. "Is it enough?"

The men at the table exchanged glances, then Brown looked at Long and said, "It's enough, Mr. Long."

"All right, then," Long said. "Drinks for everyone, Mr. McKeever."

"Yes, sir."

After Long left, Borcher and Fagen took off for a whorehouse or another saloon. They were warned not to talk about what was going on. That left McKeever and Brown together.

"Do you believe this?" Brown asked.

"He's crazy."

"Obviously."

"But he's rich."

"And you've seen his money?"

"Oh, yeah," McKeever said, nodding. "I've done work for him in the past."

"Anything this nuts?"

"No," McKeever said. "In the past it's been pretty straightforward. This is different."

"What about you and the Gunsmith?"

"What about him?"

"Ever met before?"

"No," McKeever said, "this will be the first—and last—time."

FORTY-TWO

They were all pretty exhausted from the trip, especially Sarah and Burton, so the two Brits turned in early. Their accommodations were nowhere near as nice as in some of the Eastern cities, but they didn't much care. They were asleep as soon as their heads hit their pillows.

Clint and Gallows, however, still had some life left in them. Clint was used to this kind of travel, and Gallows was unabashedly excited about being in Tombstone, the home of the O.K. Corral.

The Four Kings had a small saloon attached, nothing that could compete with saloons like the Alhambra and the Oriental, just something for the benefit of their guests.

They were seated at a table in the back of the saloon and through the front window they could see the well-lit front of the Oriental Saloon across the street.

"These places are all legendary in the East," Gallows said. "I can't believe I'm here."

"Chicago is not exactly the East," Clint said.

"My point is you've been out here, you've lived it," Gallows said. "I've only read about it."

"And you can't believe everything you read."

"Come on, Clint," Gallows said. "You were here for it. You saw it. What was it like?"

"It was bloody," Clint said, "and vicious, and mostly, it was unnecessary."

Gallows could see that Clint didn't really want to talk about it, so he backed off.

"I'm gonna take a walk around town tomorrow," he said. "Maybe go down to the O.K. Corral."

"That's fine," Clint said. "I'll stay with Sarah."

"Why?" Gallows asked. "We pretty much have established that we're not bein' followed."

"That may be," Clint said, "but there's something that we haven't established."

"And what's that?"

"There's no secret about Sarah's schedule, is there?"

"No," Gallows said. "In fact, it was published in some Eastern newspapers when they first arrived here."

"That's what I thought."

"So what haven't we established, Clint?"

"Maybe we haven't been followed since St. Louis," Clint said, "but who's to say somebody didn't get here ahead of us?"

McKeever and Brown were still in the Oriental, unware that Clint and Gallows were right across the street in the Four Kings. They were planning the kidnapping of Sarah Bernhardt from the Birdcage Theater the next night.

"What about the law?" Brown asked.

"What about 'em?" McKeever asked.

"Do we know who it is?"

"Whoever it is," McKeever said, "it ain't gonna be the Earps. Look, we're gonna snatch that little gal and be outta here before the town knows what happened."

"And what about Adams?"

"Clint Adams will be dead," McKeever said, "along with that detective and the manager, Burton. You and the boys are gonna take care of them."

"Do we really need to kill all of 'em?" Brown asked.

"When did you ever worry about killin'?" McKeever asked.

"I ain't worried about killin'," Brown said, "I'm worried about a posse."

"There's gonna be so much confusion," McKeever said, "that they won't get a posse together for a while."

"Okay," Brown said, "so you got everything figured out, except you ain't told me yet how we're gonna grab her."

"Well, then, listen up," McKeever said, "because you're gonna have to explain it to the others . . ."

Instead of walking through the saloon to the lobby of the hotel Clint and Gallows preferred to step outside and get some air.

"This is the street," Gallows said. "Allan Street. The street they all walked down."

"Jack," Clint said, "they were just men, and many of them are still alive." But not Morgan, he thought to himself, and not Doc.

"I know they were just men," Gallows said.

"Well, then, can you stop acting like some kid who just saw Hercules for the first time?"

"Who?"

"Forget it," Clint said. "I'm gonna turn in."

"Me, too."

As they walked to the front door of the hotel Gallows asked, "You gonna sit in front of her door tonight?"

"No," Clint said, "I think it's enough that we have the

rooms on either side of her. We should be able to hear if anything goes wrong."

"But we don't expect it to, right?"

As they entered the hotel lobby Clint said, "I think we've seen plenty of proof that you never can tell."

FORTY-THREE

McKeever used Frank Long's money to buy theater tickets
for all the men. All, that is, except Borcher. They had managed to get him hired by the theater to keep people from
going backstage during and after the performance. When
Borcher had gone and applied for the job, he'd been told
that they had someone to do it, and the manager had mentioned the name Peter Brant. Well, to the surprise of everyone in town except McKeever and Henry Brown, Peter
Brant suddenly went missing. The theater manager re-
membered Borcher and hired him to replace the irresponsi-
ble Brant.

And since Borcher had been hired as a guard, he was
privy to some helpful information—like where Clint
Adams and Jack Gallows would be during the performance. That information was key to McKeever's plan.
They also used Long's money to buy each of the men a de-
cent suit, so they would not stick out when they went to the
theater. And one of the reasons the Birdcage was the per-
fect place to make this play, rather than a theater back East,
is that most of the men present would be wearing a gun.

So when the performance was about to start, McKeever,
Brown, Borcher and Fagen were all in place . . .

•   •   •

Clint took up his position in one of the Birdcage's famous "birdcage" boxes on the second level. The whores usually took customers down to a basement level to do their business, but there was a time when the whores could ply their trade in the boxes, as well. Clint's box was stage right and Jack Gallows was in the box at stage left. John Burton had a seat in the first row.

Burton was not impressed by the rustic charm of the Birdcage Theater, nor was he charmed by its reputation.

"Filthy place," he said, when they walked through it. "I'm glad I only booked us in here for one night."

"I'll just be happy to say that I played here, John," Sarah told him.

"Nevertheless . . ." the Englishman said.

Clint waved to Gallows to indicate he was in his box. Gallows waved back. This would be an interesting angle from which to watch Sarah Bernhardt perform, Clint thought.

Henry Brown took up his position outside Jack Gallows's box. On the other side of the theater Fagen was outside of Clint's. Borcher was manning his post at stage right, and McKeever was seated in the second row, behind John Burton.

The curtain came up, as did the lights, and Sarah Bernhardt swept out onto the stage . . .

The Tombstone audience was no different than any other Sarah had played to during her North American tour. They loved her and rewarded her with thunderous applause at the end of the performance.

After she had gone offstage, the crowd stood and began to file out. As Burton leaned forward to stand up, a hand landed on his shoulder and pulled him back.

"I beg you pard—" he started, but something sharp jabbed him in the back, stopping him.

"Shhh." Jarrod McKeever hissed in Burton's ear. His bowie knife had gone straight through the back of Burton's seat and into his back. "It'll be all right," McKeever whispered, as he pushed the knife in deeper. Burton stiffened, but McKeever placed his other hand on Burton's shoulder and kept him where he was. McKeever continued to speak to him. To anyone watching them they looked for all the world like two men discussing the performance.

When McKeever was sure the smaller man could not get up, he withdrew the knife, surreptitiously wiped it clean on the left shoulder of Burton's jacket, then stood and approached the stage. As the last of the people were filing out, heading for the saloon, or a restaurant, or, perhaps, downstairs for a whore, Borcher stepped aside to let McKeever backstage, then followed.

Clint watched the crowd file out, then brought his eyes back to the first row, where Burton had been sitting. He saw Burton begin to rise, only to be stopped by the man behind him. It looked as if the two were having a conversation, then the second abruptly stood and went backstage. The man whose job it was to stop him was either very bad at it or had no intentions of ever stopping him.

Burton didn't move. That alone would have alerted Clint that something was wrong, but there was more. The second man looked like the man he'd seen prowling about in the Fox Theater, the man Jack Gallows had said might be Jarrod McKeever.

He turned quickly and reached for the doorknob of the door to his box. It turned, but the door would not open. He pushed again, but still it would not yield. He turned to look down at Burton, who had not yet moved, and was now slumping a bit to one side.

Now he stood and waved frantically to catch Gallows's attention, but even as he did that he could see the detective pushing on the door to his own box. Suddenly, Gallows turned and their eyes locked. They both looked down to the first floor and saw two more men rush backstage. That made four men who were now backstage with Sarah Bernhardt.

Clint wondered if he could leap from his box to the stage without snapping his ankle as John Wilkes Booth had at the Ford Theater after shooting Abraham Lincoln.

It was a chance he was going to have to take.

FORTY-FOUR

When the two men burst into Sarah Bernhardt's dressing room she had not yet removed her dress.

"What is the meaning of this?" she demanded.

"Come on, lady," McKeever said. "Somebody wants to see you."

"Who?"

"A big fan."

She backed away from the big man while the smaller man stared at her from the door.

"I am not going."

"Yeah," McKeever said, "you are."

He grabbed her wrist hard enough to force her to cry out and dragged her from the room. Outside she had to step over a fallen stagehand. There were two more men there, but it was obvious rescue was not on their agenda. She searched frantically for Clint Adams but there was no sign of him.

"This way," Borcher said, because he knew where the back door was.

McKeever followed, pulling Sarah along behind him. At the door he turned and handed Sarah off to Henry Brown.

"Get her to Long," he said. "I'll meet you there."

"But—"

"This is my part, Henry," he said. "Adams is gonna come after her. That blocked door will slow him down, but it ain't gonna stop him."

"Okay," Brown said. "See you there."

Behind his hotel Frank Long sat in the front seat of a buckboard. Driving the thing would be difficult for him, but he planned on having one of the other men do it. Tied to the rear of the buckboard were four horses. He, McKeever and the men would proceed directly to Fairbank, where he and Sarah Bernhardt would begin their journey back East.

He really hadn't thought it out much further than that. The most important thing was to have her in his possession. This obsession had driven him to irrational actions that a sane mind would not have considered.

Clint leaped to the stage while Jack Gallows chose to dangle from his box, then release his hold. They both escaped with no injury and looked at each other.

"Go out the front!" Clint shouted. "I'll go backstage!"

"Right!"

Clint ran to the wings and into the backstage area. Gallows took off up the aisle to run out the front door.

Outside Gallows stopped. Some of the audience members were still milling about, but there was no sign of Sarah Bernhardt. He paused only long enough to ask some of them to get a doctor to help an injured man in the theater. Then he ducked down the alley next to the theater and started running for the back.

Clint spotted the fallen stagehand in front of Sarah's dressing room and knew the worst had happened. There was only one other way for them to get out, so he headed for the back door without stopping to check the man. He hadn't stopped to check on John Burton. He only hoped that neither man would die because of it.

As he reached the back door he saw a man leaning against it, picking at his nails with a bowie knife. He stopped and faced the man.

"You made it," the man said. "I knew that door wouldn't hold you long."

"You're McKeever?"

The man look surprised.

"I'm impressed."

"Where's the woman?"

"On her way, I'd say."

"On her way where?"

McKeever shrugged.

"To wherever my employer chooses to take her. You see, I don't care. I only took the job because of you."

"Which hotel?"

"What?"

"Which hotel is he in?"

McKeever dropped his bowie knife. It struck the floor point first and vibrated there.

"Forget it," he said. "This is me and you—"

Normally, Clint allowed the other man in a gunfight every chance to back down. He even went so far as to allow the man the first move. But these were not normal circumstances. He didn't have the time to waste. He simply drew and fired before McKeever even knew what had happened.

"Wha—" the man said, as the bullet struck him in the chest.

Clint ran for the door, pushed McKeever to the side, where he fell to the floor, dead, a stunned look still on his face. In the dim recesses of his brain, just before he died came the thought, "I wasn't ready."

• • •

Clint burst through the back door and came face-to-face
with Jack Gallows.

"Shit!" he swore.

"I heard a shot."

"I killed one," he said. "It was McKeever."

"McKeever?"

"Obviously, he got here ahead of us. There's three
more, Jack, and they have Sarah."

"Where are they taking her?"

"I don't know," Clint said. "McKeever said his employer wanted Sarah."

"For wha—"

"We don't have time to wonder," Clint said. "If they
didn't come out that alley you just came through, then they
went this way, behind the buildings. Come on."

"Where?"

"We just have to keep moving while we're trying to figure that out."

FORTY-FIVE

The three men told Sarah they would kill her if she cried out. In her frightened state she knew that they dared not do that or they would never get paid. She allowed them to drag her along until they reached the back of the Palace hotel. Sarah didn't give the men any trouble crossing the street, so even though there were some people on the street returning home from the theater, they gave the actress and her accosters no notice.

Henry Brown yanked Sarah down the alley next to the Palace, followed by Borcher and Fagen. When they got to the back of the hotel they saw Frank Long sitting on the seat of the buckboard. From there, at least, he could look down at them.

"Where's McKeever?" he asked.

"He stayed behind to take care of Adams," Brown said.

Long didn't speak again. He was staring at Sarah Bernhardt. She, in turn, was staring up at him.

"Hello, Miss Bernhardt," he said. "At last we meet."

"I know you," she said.

"Ah, you remember. I am flattered."

"In . . . Philadelphia."

"Yes."

"You came backstage to see me," she said. "You asked me to dinner."

"You rebuffed me."

"I . . . had another engagement."

Frank Long laughed.

"You don't think I know why women reject me unless I pay them?" he asked. He stood up in the buckboard, straightened to his full three foot six.

"N-no," she said, but she was lying. She had turned down his offer because he was a dwarf. She felt guilty afterward, but what could she do? She could never be interested in a man his size.

"Put her in the back," he said to Brown. "One of you drive the buckboard."

"What about McKeever?" Brown asked.

"If he's not here now he's not coming. It means Adams killed him. We have to get going."

"But—" Brown started.

"I'll split his share evenly among you," Long said.

"Get in the buckboard, lady!" Brown said.

As Clint and Gallows reached the street they heard the sound of approaching horses, but they couldn't see them. Then, from the mouth of the alley, a buckboard appeared, followed by two men on horseback, and a third, unridden horse.

There was no way for Frank Long and his men to get Sarah Bernhardt out of town without riding down Allan Street. When they all exploded from the alley Clint shouted to Jack Gallows, "Other side of the street."

Gallows reacted immediately, running to the far side of the street. Both men had their guns drawn. As the buckboard approached them, followed by the mounted men, they were able to catch them in a cross fire. The two men on horseback had their guns out and were firing. Clint and

Gallows took cover—Clint behind a barrel, Gallows a horse trough—and returned fire. The two men on horses suddenly flew off them, as if tugged from behind, but they had actually been pushed off by striking bullets.

That left the man driving the buckboard, who had his hands full trying to control the spooked horses. Clint and Gallows both stepped from cover and fired together. The man was struck from both sides. The equal impact kept him from sliding off the seat.

Jack Gallows leaped out in front of the horses, which had not yet been able to get up a head of steam. He waved his arms and the team slowed enough for him to grab them and bring them to a stop.

Clint ran around behind the buckboard and looked in. What he saw almost struck him funny. Sarah was curled up in one corner of the buckboard and in the other he saw a very small man.

"Sarah!" Clint called.

She opened her eyes, saw Clint and scrambled to him. He pulled her from the buckboard and she stood behind him. Gallows had gotten the horses to quiet down and joined the two at the back of the buckboard.

"What the—" Gallows said. "I know this little man from Philadelphia, don't I, Sarah?"

"Yes," she said. "I turned down an invitation to dinner. Apparently, he thought that enough provocation to track me down and try to kidnap me."

Frank Long—known in Philadelphia as Francis Long, a banker and a real estate agent of great wealth—managed to get to his feet and face the threesome.

"Gentlemen," he said, "I have a great deal of money and a lot of power back East. We can make a deal."

Clint and Gallows both pointed their guns at the diminutive man, and Clint said, "In case you haven't noticed, Mr. Long, we're not in the East."

• • •

The death of John Burton did not put an end to Sarah Bernhardt's North American tour.

"He would have wanted me to finish," she told Clint and Gallows.

As for Frank Long, he had been thrown into the Tombstone jail to await trial. Clint and Gallows agreed to stay in touch by telegraph and return to testify when it was necessary. Of course, Clint thought, before then the little man might be able to buy his way back home with his money. Justice was not always blind, but sometimes it saw green. By that time, however, Sarah Bernhardt would likely be on the way home.

"I'm not gonna take that chance," Gallows said, on the morning they were to leave Tombstone, several days after the incident.

"What do you mean?"

"I'm gonna stay with you as far as Denver," Gallows said, "and then I'll come back. I'll catch a train back to Philadelphia, if I have to, but I'm gonna see that he doesn't get away with this. Too many people died because of him."

They were waiting outside the hotel for Sarah to appear. All the bags had been loaded onto the stage. John Burton had been buried on boot hill. They all thought that was kind of ironic and would have appealed to the man.

"I wouldn't get my hopes up, Jack," Clint said. "He does have a lot of money."

"I also think he's stark-raving mad," Gallows said.

Clint rubbed his jaw as Sarah appeared in the hotel doorway and said, "Yeah, that might just work in your favor."

Watch for

AMAZON GOLD

289th novel in the exciting GUNSMITH series
from Jove

Coming in January!

J. R. ROBERTS

THE GUNSMITH

GIANT ACTION! GIANT ADVENTURE!

THE GUNSMITH

GIANT

GIANT WESTERNS FEATURING THE GUNSMITH

THE GHOST OF BILLY THE KID
0-515-13622-0

LITTLE SURESHOT AND THE WILD WEST SHOW
0-515-13851-7

DEAD WEIGHT
0-515-14028-7

J799

Explore the exciting Old West with one of the men who made it wild!